By Andrew Dolha

The Guardian: A Trace Anderson Adventure
Void Jumper (Forthcoming, Fall 2014)

TABLE OF CONTENTS

For my beautiful family...

The Guardian
by Andrew Dolha

ONE: Good Morning

"Ack! Ackkk! Aaaaakkkkkaaaa, ack ackkkk!" Pain lanced through Trace's semi-conscious brain. The reverberate clang of a jackhammer offered no respite, jarring him awake from where he slept in his Air Stream trailer he had affectionately named Tank. A little beaten and bruised, Tank had housed him over the years on every construction job he'd taken. It was a place he called home, a safe refuge from the rigors of reality, normally.

This morning, however, Tank was an echo chamber, torturing Trace with the sound of a jackhammer ricocheting off the interior. He didn't like waking up at the best of times. He was typically gun-shy opening his eyelids on a new morning because he was never quite sure of where he might be or what might have happened the night before.

Trace sat up, the movement causing waves of nausea, steadied himself and cautiously stood. *So far so good.* He then shuffled across the room, following the aroma of coffee, thankful that he had remembered to set the coffee pot before going out on an evening of homemade grappa shots with the boys after work. He made his way to the door and opened it to reveal 'the hole'. A two-acre pit, being dug to house the tallest building in the world. This was his newest baby. *I dig holes, man.* He had been hired by Janks Incorporated to oversee the construction of the foundation, from stem to stern. This morning, with his head full of crap and pain, he couldn't help thinking he was getting too old for the big projects.

The jackhammer pounded on. Trace felt like curling into a ball, which would not be easy for his stupidly large 6'4" body, he towered over many off the men in his employ, who were beginning to pour onto the worksite. A good crew, most had worked with Trace since he started contracting for himself. He was perversely happy to see that some of the men looked a little worse for wear from their own reveling last night.

He made his way carefully down Tank's steps toward the sound. He didn't have to go far. Right beside Tank, behind the onsite office trailer, Trace found the offender, or rather, offenders. One of his favorite sub-crews, Johns, Sax, and Smithy, better known as the Three Amigos, sat on spools of wire with coffees and wearing ear muffs. Beside them, a young new muscle-bound recruit named Bobby was frantically trying to break up a piece of concrete with a jackhammer. The Three Amigos watched Trace with shit-eating grins as he gingerly approached the operator.

Trace yelled. "BOBBY! BOBBY! FOR CHIRSTSAKES, BOBBY! SHUT THAT BLOODY THING OFF!"

But young Bobby didn't hear over the noise making the grins from the Amigos bigger. Trace's head was about to explode as he finally got close enough to hit the kill switch on the generator. Then, silence. Bliss. Bobby looked up startled and confused at Trace's stormy face. The Three Amigos exploded with laughter.

"Hey Trace, what's up? My daddy's hooch too much for ya?", Sax said, barely able to talk, "Can't hold it like you used to eh, old man?"

Bobby chimed in, a worried look on his face from pissing off the boss. "I'm sorry Trace, they told me that I should get this done. That you were pissed that it didn't get done yesterday."

Trace considered his options for revenge on the three amigos.

Trace clapped Bobby on the shoulder. "No worries, Bobby. You did good work here, and since you took the initiative, this morning you can take it easy working on the supply list. These three here are going in the pit."

Trace's triumphant smile met the agonized groans of the Three Amigos.

"Let's go boys, unless you want to clear latrines...."

<<>>

The pit, as it was so lovingly called, was a half-acre across and about just as deep. Blasting, digging, and clearing was a slow process. A hundred men, split into crews of various sizes, worked under Trace's command performing a variety of jobs. He was proud of the work they did. They were all professionals and the best in the business at their jobs. Trace knew the megalith that would eventually be built into this giant hole, would be on firm footing once it started skyward, easily dwarfing the Burj Khalifa in Dubai, clocking in at around 4000 feet. He wondered though, as he made his way down the pit elevator in the mid-afternoon sun, how long it would be before some egotistical architect would trump that. He wondered just how high a building could go, and if it was worth the effort. Trace shook his head as he thought of the number of years the project would be in the making. He was thankful that he just had to make the hole to house it.

That afternoon, Trace found the Three Amigos's crew pounding away at the larger blasted boulders with jackhammers. Sweat pouring off of them as they baked and labored in the hot sun. They stopped on his approach, breathing heavily.

"Hey pussy, you gonna get dirty today or what?" Smithy called out.

Johns spat impressively onto the rubble he had made. "Nah, he doesn't want to get his manicure all fucked up."

Sax, sweating more than looked healthy, chimed in. "Yeah, he wants to stay all pretty for us."

Trace laughed along. "Hey Sax, you drown your old lady when you're doing the nasty with all that sweat? You should collect some in a jar, should be about 40 proof."

Johns and Smithy chuckled as Sax affectionately gave Trace the finger, and then hoisted the jack to another boulder. But just as he reached for the trigger to turn it on, the ground collapsed beneath him.

Instant pandemonium. Sax disappeared through a crack in the Earth about five feet wide. Johns and Smithy managed to jump back and fall along the edge. Trace was knocked forward toward the hole, but managed to grab one of the Jack cords as he fell. When the dust settled, he was hanging, tangled in power cords, about 10 feet above the floor of a cavern that was not there a minute before. Beneath he could hear groaning. "Sax, you okay?" Trace called into the darkness, his voice frantic.

"Shit! I think I broke my fucking leg!" Sax yelled back, his voice wracked with pain.

"Don't worry, man, we'll get you out of there," Trace called down, trying to sound calm.

Johns and Smithy were already springing into action. Within minutes they managed to pull Trace up by the cord, get a rope and harness around him, then drop him back down to look after Sax. As Trace was being lowered, he took in the immense size of the cavern. *Damn thing isn't supposed to be here.* It didn't register on any of his seismic reports or grading surveys, which was impossible because it was huge. This was going to be a major setback in an already tight schedule. Not to mention a man injured. *Fuck, fuck, fuck.*

Trace reached the floor of the cavern and moved quickly to where Sax lay.

"Damn, shit, bloody hell. So much for my dance lessons." Sax growled between his teeth.

"No worries, buddy, I'll dance with your wife," Trace joked.

"The hell you will. She don't like nobody sweating on her but me."

"Then let's get you out of here."

Half an hour later the crew had managed to hoist Sax out of the cavern to the medics who were just arriving above. Trace stayed below to take stock of the size of the hole within a hole. He had ordered a stop to all work above, in case the roof decided to collapse.

Smithy called down. "You shouldn't be down there, man. This whole thing could come in on you."

Trace knew he was right, but when did that ever stop him? "Just a couple minutes, I want to see the size of our new pain in the ass."

Trace walked away from the opening, the light from his flashlight disappearing into the gloom beyond. The hole descended downwards as he walked deeper, the ceiling a thick layer of solid rock. As his flashlight played over the surface, he gasped at what he saw.

He was in an immense dome, over 100 feet high and spreading out into dark all around. The walls were smooth and oddly reflective. *What the hell is this place?* He looked back at the hole behind and above him, thankful that no one was seriously hurt. It could have been much worse. It could have been one of the big excavators, or a whole group of men. Only thing to do was to blast it all away. In some ways it would probably save time, less ground to move. He started to feel better and even optimistic that he could turn a bad situation to his advantage. He continued deeper into the chamber toward the center, as he did his flashlight slid over a pair of eyes.

What the...?

Trace let out a short, surprised grunt of terror. Heart pounding, he fixed the beam back. A gigantic statue of a man had been placed on a platform in the middle of the chamber. It was huge, about fifteen feet high, carved from a block of black stone. It was not the honor-a-war-hero kind of statue, like you see in parks and stuff. This was a statue of body that has been frozen in time, it seemed, in a moment of extreme duress. Arms outstretched, body coiled, like the guy had been warding off an attack from all around him. The face was hideous, snarling mouth half opened, nose twisted in a sneer...but the eyes. The eyes were intense with hatred, even carved from solid rock they seemed, somehow, to be watching him, popping out in stark relief to the rock surrounding them.

Trace couldn't believe what he'd just stumbled upon. He wasn't the type to get freaked out, ever. But this face, with those eyes, raised the hairs on the back of his neck and sent a cold chill down his spine.

He had a feeling things were about to get very complicated.

The following morning Trace was up early. He had shut down the site and roped off the area around the cave-in. He put in two calls after that. The first was a protocol call to health and safety as well as a quick call to the city regarding archeological finds. Health and safety would want to make sure the site was safe and that proper precautions were in place for the workers. Many cities that he had worked in had started to require companies to do due diligence when it came to finding anything of possible historical significance. The fines for not doing so were substantial. The last call was to Chuck Veeman, the business rep for the investors at Janks, who were meeting this morning to discuss the situation after Trace had emailed them a cursory report.

Chuck Veeman was a corpulent hothead who hadn't, Trace figured, eaten anything green in years. His face sat on several chin pillows and he was constantly sweating hard, even in the winter. He had beady, intelligent pig-eyes and had been married six times. Trace was sure Chuck had eaten his last wife. He had to admit, however, he did like working for Chuck. He was a bastard, but he was a hard worker and got the job done.

The Skype call connected and Chuck's blob face filled Trace's computer screen.

"Hey Chuck...how goes Weight Watchers?"

Chuck did not seem amused. "Ha, Ha, fuck you. Jesus, Trace, what the hell is going on over there?"

"I thought I went over that in my email to Janks."

"Don't be a smart-ass. I mean the archeology department."

"I'm required to call them. What did you want me to do?"

"I wanted you to say nothing. A thing like this could shut us down indefinitely."

"Yeah, but you've got see this thing, Chuck...it's..." He was at a loss for words and resorted to vague hand signals in front of the camera. "I mean, have you seen the pictures?"

"Yeah, I saw the pictures. Creepy, oooo aaaa. Some twisted bastard from a billion years ago has demons. Guess what? I've got demons too. They are the Chair and the board of Janks Inc. So, I wouldn't give a flying fart if it were the arc of the covenant down there. We are losing thousands every day of shutdown. I want you to get down there and blow it up."

"What!? Are you nuts?"

"Tell them it was an accident. Blow the hole and get the job going again."

"No way, Chuck."

"Then you are on the outs, Trace."

If there is one thing Trace didn't like it was being threatened. He glared at Chuck, swallowed his rage, and snapped, "Fine. Get yourself another hole-digger. Good luck, Chuck!"

Silence. Chuck stared at Trace, beady eyes streaming imaginary bullets through the computer. "You know I can't do that. You're the only one who's got the cred to do this job."

"Thanks for noticing. But I'm still not blowing shit up and lying about it."

Chuck blew through his cheeks, making him look like some scary exotic fish. "Okay fine, sorry. I'm sorry, Okay? I'm getting peed on from above, I'm a little stressed. The archeology department is coming over today. Can you at least try to get them to move the damn thing or something? Anything that does not cost us time."

Trace smiled good-naturedly at him. "Sure. I'll see what I can do. Stay away from stress-eating, okay Chuck?"

Chuck nodded, but didn't take the bait. "Great advice. Fuck you. Goodbye." He pushed a button in front of him and the Skype call ended.

Trace stared at the blank screen for a few minutes trying to gather his thoughts. *What the hell was that thing down there?* In all his years he'd never seen anything like it. He'd dug up a few old things, some pottery, a few bones, one time a cool rusted sword, but never anything like this. He was genuinely intrigued by the find; something different from the grind of construction. *As long as it doesn't bog me down too long.* He hoped the archeology department sent would send over someone who could answer his questions and come up with a quick solution.

Two hours later Trace was standing on the edge of the cavern with the most beautiful woman he'd ever seen.

TWO: An Angel with Red Hair

Her name was Agnes. A totally ugly name, in complete contrast to the curvy, red-haired woman standing beside Trace. Tall, around five ten, strong featured, full lips, noble nose, and piercing violet eyes. She was wearing tight jeans, wrapping ample hips and long legs, which ended in no-nonsense hiking boots. A somewhat baggy faded plaid shirt was unbuttoned just enough for modesty, but still showed the shape of generous, and the edge of a hot pink lace bra. Slung over her shoulder she casually held onto a short leather jacket.

Trying to hide what he was sure was an audible gulp, Trace thrust his hand out to her, calluses contrasting with her silky skin. She consumed Trace with one thorough look from her violet eyes, summed him up, and categorized him in a way he found both violating and alluring. Trace couldn't help but feel she had found him lacking. *Dear God, she thinks I'm an idiot.*

"Trace Anderson, just call me Trace." He spread his best smile across his face like a big dollop of cream cheese across a toasted bagel.

She smiled back, benignly, but still looked vaguely disgusted. Even so, he found her captivating. She had a mouth that begged to be open and against him, and a pony-tail restraining a heap of dark red hair that asked to be yanked, gently but firmly. Curves like a Monte Carlo roadway. *What I wouldn't give to race around that track,* Trace thought. *Why is that shiny stuff women put on their lips so enticing, so alluring?*

Trace loved to sleep with women, and he was of the opinion they shared the mutual consideration. He had had a few long-term girlfriends, at least three to six months, but his work always screwed that up, or he did, or she did. He was not a conquest guy, notches-on-the-belt sort of thing; carved names on a sad tree - no, he didn't keep a tally - but he had a photographic memory of all those who had shared some nocturnal time with him. They haunted him for some reason, late at night, in dreams. Not because he felt guilty or anything, he was always upfront and always told them his intentions before they did the deed. *No,* He thought, *it's not guilt, but something else.* Something he would deal with at another time. At the moment, he couldn't seem to form any kind of coherent thought, then realized he was still shaking this goddess's hand. She had to disengage herself first.

"Agnes Argwhistle" she said. "Hello, Mr. Anderson".

Trace couldn't help but twitch a smile about her name, in complete contrast to the lush lady who owned it. Argwhistle sounded to him like a pirate call, or the sound a tin flute player made when he died. Trace knew he had done a poor job disguising his mirth over her name because she launched into a grumpy Coles notes explanation of its origins.

"I'm named after a late, great-aunt who had a lot of cash. My Dad hoped to get a little rubbed off on him so he named me after her. Instead, the old dear left her millions to a budgie named Clive Otis. That will is still stuck in probation, contested in the courts."

She chuckled at the foolishness of her family as she strode toward the pit. Trace trailed behind her like a wasp to a luscious, red strawberry.

By the time they arrived at the taped-off zone, Trace had managed to retrieve some of his sanity and check his hormones as he bumbled through a narrative of the cave-in.

"Let's go in then," she said as Trace got her fitted with a hardhat, which looked stupidly good on her. They then made their way down the ladder and scaffold that had been set up for access to the pit below. Gravel crunched underneath their feet as they moved through the cavern

amidst Agnes's 'oohs' and 'ahhs', while Trace played the
travel guide, yacking and flipping his arms to the he-man
narrative of his great adventure. By the time he'd finished
the story of the cave-in they were at the coup de gras of the
underground tour: the giant statue.

Agnes's eyes shone with an excited fervor. "Wow.
That is amazing. I can't believe it."

Trace wished, in that moment, she would one day
shine those orbs on him in the same way.

"So what is it?" Trace asked, trying to sound like he
had a clue, but only needed a few more puzzle pieces to
bounce off. "I mean, where's it from? Looks Egyptian, sort
of."

Trace knew in a moment that that was the wrong thing
to say, because he got a sideways twitch from Agnes's
lower lip. When she replied, she sounded like his fifth
grade teacher.

"No, Mr. Anderson, this is nothing like Egyptian.
Look at the carvings. Too detailed and in full relief, the
smoothness of the rock suggests advanced carving tools,
beyond advanced. You'd be hard-pressed to make a surface
like that, even today."

"Wait a minute, this thing *is* old isn't it? It wasn't just
put here recently?"

Trace shook his head, not comprehending, and realized
that he was actually enjoying the mystery she proposed.

"How could it have come from advanced machinery?"

"There are more things in heaven and Earth,
Horatio..." Agnes mused, her lower lip a pillow Trace
ached for.

"What's Hamlet got to do with it?" He asked. This time
the surprise on her face was genuine and pointed in Trace's
direction. He felt waves of genuine pleasure at her half-
smile and widening irises. *Cool. Perhaps I'm not so dumb
after all, hey, beautiful lady?*

Agnes stared at him for a moment, making him feel as though he was being dissected.

"Yes, Mr. Anderson," she drawled, extending the word 'yeeees' out so that it actually sounded like no. "We don't know everything, do we?"

Her voice and arched-eyebrow-challenge, brought him back to his high school English teacher, Mrs. Hengold. She had told Trace he wouldn't amount to anything.

The memory made him wince. He worked his ass off in school, needing to prove Hengold wrong. When he graduated, he went up to her and confronted her.

"I will amount to more than you could possibly imagine, lady".

She stared at him for a while, a semi-half smile on her face, unreadable.

"Time will tell, I suppose, Mr. Anderson." She said, "But I don't hold out hope."

Her ignorance lit a fire under Trace and he started working right out of high school, dropping out of the lame college he was unexcited about and lying about his age to find work on the rigs. Then he moved on to every construction job imaginable. He had practiced almost every trade and was a master of many. Brick laying, roofing, framing, landscaping, electronics, you name it, he's done it. Bought the t-shirt. He considered himself sort of a practical rain man, an idiot savant in the construction trade. The thought of his English teacher's low opinion of him, though, still made Trace clench his jaw in shame.

Trace realized he had been staring at Agnes, who had a puzzled look on her face and seemed about to say something, but Trace turned away from her, leading her closer in to examine the statue. Agnes started bubbling forth with a string of archeology talk that Trace was sure gave the boys in the lab a jolt of pleasure but, frankly, left him in the cold, probably because he didn't really have a clue what half the words she was spouting meant. *She's beautiful AND smart, and I won't amount to anything. I'm doomed.*

"Mr. Anderson! Look here*!" Still on the last name.* Trace looked over to where Agnes was excitedly pointing.

She was running her hands over small markings that had been carved into the base of the statue, *long slender soft moisturizer hands*...Trace shook his head clear and made his way over to to take in the markings she seemed so thrilled with. *Looks like chicken scrawl to me,* Trace thought, but he feigned interest.

"What do they mean? Are you familiar with this kind of writing?" Now, Trace knew he sounded completely academic with that question, but Agnes didn't seem to notice. She just shook her head and from inside a jacket pocket produced a pocket camera. *Candid shots, awesome,* Trace thought.

The digital camera came to life under her hands as she clicked and flashed her way around the statue. Trace managed to 'accidentally' get caught in the frame a few times, nonchalantly flexing his triceps.

"I've never seen anything that even comes close to this!"

Agnes's voice got breathy, and then went up an octave as she spoke. *Oh that I could be the cause of such throaty excitement.* Agnes packed up her camera and looked at him with worry.

"This may be one of the most important discoveries ever unearthed."

Trace's reverie was shattered at the implications of what she was saying. In his mind he saw this place covered with archeologists armed with little brushes, excavating for years, inch by inch. *This will not do.* Trace knew he had to find a way out. Regardless of her perfection, she needed to get him out of the jam with the company.

"Yeah, sure and your and my name can totally be in on the find," Trace chuckled and tried to shoot down her eye-roll with his cute grin. Almost never failed. Almost.

"But listen Agnes, trust me, no one loves a find of the century more than me, but unfortunately I've got a hole to dig and a company spending millions to get it dug. Cool though this is, I have a schedule and a president breathing down my neck."

Dark clouds seemed to roll across her eyes in a terrifying instant. They were still beautiful, but now they were scary beautiful.

"Mr. Anderson," she paused to clear her already clear voice, "while I appreciate the creation of giant glass and steel phalluses to compensate for the shortcomings of small-minded companies, surely you realize the importance of what has been discovered here."

Doomed.

"I get it Agnes, I really do. Would make a great write up in Archeology Today, Weekly, Last Century, or whatever. But you have to help me out here." An idea popped into his head as he spoke. "Maybe we can just move this thing out of here? I've got a lot of heavy machines and strong men at my disposal. I'd be more than happy to fire them up for you."

Agnes looked at him with patronizing impatience.

"Very kind of you, but it's not just the statue, it's the entire site that has to be excavated and explored. There may be more things here than we know. I'm afraid I have the authority to make this difficult for your company." She paused as her face washed over with helplessness. In that instant Trace found he wanted to be her superhero. "Please, Mr. Anderson, I'm going to need someone on my side here."

'Please.' Shit. I'm double doomed.

Lawsuits and demonstrators and 'Kum By Ya' flashed before Trace's eyes, not to mention his once-brilliant career. Her earnest eyes were worse than her scary eyes. He felt helpless before her pleading expression.

"Well, I'll talk to them, but they'll want something, an expedited archeological excavation, or something. How long are we talking here?"

Agnes thought for a moment as she looked over the site. "Well, most digs take years..."

"Sorry, sister, that will not work with them," Trace cut in, "it's a tight spot and if we get the lawyers involved then nobody will be moving down here, my guys or yours."

Agnes's face darkened at the implied threat, but her anger didn't seem directed at him. She raised her hand to forestall any more discussion.

"Let's see what they say and take it from there." Her face then took on a cute questioning look, "Who knows maybe they will understand?"

"Oh, sure, they'll be full of sunshine and smiles." Trace said. "Come on, let's get out of here."

It was clear where Chuck stood on the matter. His face once again filled Trace's computer on Skype.

"What are you, a dick-head? Are you insane? Months? Anderson, what in the name of shit are you talking about? I want that friggin' cavern blown up. We'll give them a week and we can haul the fucking statue out of there and we can turn it into a fountain for the front of the building."

Trace tried to reason with him. "Chuck, listen. I don't think that's going to work..."

Chuck cut him off, "I don't give a helicopter fart what you think, dick weed. Blow the fucker. Or you will be the one not working."

It was Trace's turn to get pissed. "I already told you, I'm not blowing anything up for you, Chuck."

"Gosh, Trace, you're denial makes me want you all the more. Fine, then you can tell the suits at Janks Inc. that we're throwing away many millions of dollars because of a hunk of rock and your shot at a hot archeologist."

"That was cold man, I..." Chuck gave him the finger and then switched off. *Love the Internet, eh?* Trace thought, *No awkward goodbyes on the electronic highway, no sir. The swine probably didn't have his pants on.* Trace stabbed at the keys on his keyboard. Frustration never sat well with him, he needed to get out. He grabbed his jacket and keys and stormed out of his trailer into the early evening in search of a way to vent.

Chuck was pissed to be sure. He liked Trace, had worked with him on a couple of jobs. He was an honest asshole and they were hard to come by in this business. Chuck clicked the Skype number for Harry Barniker, President of Janks in charge of development, and within a few minutes his mean 'fuck you' face was filling Chuck's screen.

"Well?"

"Sorry to bother you Mr. Barniker but that situation down at the pit has gotten worse. Seems an archeologist..."

"Solve it."

"Yes, sir you see..."

"SOLVE it."

"Any idea how you'd like me to do that Mr. Barn..."

"I don't pay myself Chuck, I pay you. Are we clear on the scenario?"

"Yep. Crystal, sir."

"Good. Get it done. I want the operation up and running in two days."

"That's not a lot of time..."

"Solve *it*."

The screen went blank. Chuck realized he was breathing hard and sweating even more than usual, like he'd been running. Something he hadn't done in years. He looked down at his desk. A succulent Boston cream donut reached out its caring smell to him. He thought of resisting, but resisted the thought. *Resistance is futile.* Like a lizard sucking in a fly, Chuck swooped the donut whole into his mouth with a quick movement of his meaty hand. Within moments he felt the temporary hit of pleasure calm his nerves. He would hate himself later, but now it was time to solve this shit-storm

      Chuck punched the screen again. A pasty rodent named Eddy Smiter appeared on the screen. Smiter was the sanitation manager on site. Good job for a little shit

      "Mr. Layton, you're up late." Eddy's beady eyes darted around the screen.

      The hit from the donut was wearing off faster than usual. Chuck had an irrational urge to reach inside the screen and smack the little twerp. Instead, he forced a smile onto his face.

      "Yes. Yes I am, Eddy, my job never ends. I need a little favor from you."

      Eddy Smiter was not a ladies man. He was a rodent. He sat in the dingy bar Chuck Layton had told him to meet at. Eddy had been watching a big tough make moves on a local peroxide. She was cold and indifferent at first, but within fifteen minutes the guy had her giggling and play-hitting him. Big bastard, the kind Eddy hated. Big hands, big muscles, granite face, big loud booming voice, laugh like an erupting volcano. Fifteen minutes after the giggling, he had his hand on her skinny ass and was leaning in close. Then they left, she rubbing herself all over him like a bottle of sun tan lotion on a side of beef.

If Eddy had his way he'd love to watch the big bastard flat on his ass pleading for the beating to stop. Yeah, that would be great, and then he'd get the girl. Eddy would take her home and watch her wriggle and writhe on top of him. Great fantasy, but Eddy was not delusional. He knew he smelled of his sanitation job. He knew he was pasty white and small. He'd been weasel-sized his whole life. His own father had called him mouse. His friends: Cockroach. Nice name: Mr. Weasel Mouse Cockroach the Third at your service. A soft bitter chuckle scraped through his throat as he sucked back the rest of his beer.

"Let me get you another." Eddy almost choked on the last of his swill as a hand came down on his shoulder.

"Eddy Smiter." Chuck Layton consumed the chair beside Eddy with his enormous ass and ordered two beers. Layton smiled at Eddy, the half-smile of the ill-at-ease which made him look to Eddy like he was pondering eating Eddy's head. Eddy gulped mentally as Layton continued.

"So I'm going to make this simple for you, Smiter. I need you to do a little job for me. Real quiet, real easy. You up for that?"

"What kind of thing, Mr. Layton?"

Twenty minutes later Eddy had been filled in, and had a wad full of cash stuffed in his pocket to boot. Maybe he could get himself one of those skinny-assed women to take notice of him. He could act the big shot, impress, with a roll like that....

"So are we clear on the details Mr. Smiter?"

Eddy nodded the 'yes mister' as Layton peeled himself out of the bar seat.

"Remember, my job is to make sure the pit is clear for the night. Yours is to set the accident and get us all back to work."

Eddy watched the rotund man leave. He hated the fat fucker, but was glad for the bonus assignment thrown his way. *Be nice to screw over Trace Anderson, that was for sure*; another big asshole that Eddy hated. The bar door opened again and a middle-aged won't-let-it-go woman sauntered in; big boobs and a skinny, sagging ass. Eddy felt confident he could make time with her. He felt confident all over. He fingered the roll of cash in his jacket pocket. Yes sir, might be his lucky night.

THREE: Warm Nights

The night was warm and Trace was in the mood to party. He knew he had no business taking an evening off while the clock ran down on the dilemma of the pit, but he felt so helpless being the middleman. He had dropped the bomb on Agnes about the nonplussed bosses, but told her that at least he had managed to hold them off for a while. She had smiled at him like an indulgent owner to a training dog. The least he could do was ask her out to, you know, smooth things over. She brushed him off like dandruff, and told him in a coldly professional tone that the morning would be a great time to get together - to work. *Strikeout.*

Trace was sure it wasn't his looks. At 40, his body was still fit and agile. He didn't consider himself to be an Adonis, but not far off. Trace could have been an actor, but that would have meant hanging out with self-important idiots. He was in a play once in high school. His mom pushed him to do it. He ended up playing Sky in the musical Guys and Dolls. Trace couldn't sing, act, or dance and most of his buddies thought he was a total ass-wipe for doing it, until they saw the number of girls he got to hang out with. The cast suddenly filled up fast with testosterone-drunk boys, much to the delight of his drama teacher Mrs. Taylor. She was about a million years old and had been teaching for two million years, but she was still kind of hot. *Strange where seventeen-year-old hormones will lead you.*

The memory made Trace chuckle to himself and he shrugged off Agnes's rejection as he arrived at the Three Amigo's hangout, the upper floor of a rundown Victorian on the edge of town. As he opened the door, the wafting aroma of Sax's Grandpa's homemade grappa assailed his nostrils and threatened to uncouple his meal from its resting place. Sax told him his grandpa made it from the leftover grape pulp after making his wine. It came in around 120 proof and could also be used to remove paint, Trace figured. Ten shots in and a half an hour later, Trace didn't care or notice. *Good night, Irene.*

Eddy waited until Trace, that big bastard, left that shit-box trailer he called home, before moving down to the pit. The rest of the crew had buggered off for the night leaving Eddy to his work. He tripped once on a small rock and jarred loose a tooth. His wrists were raw from where the broad he'd picked up the night before had cuffed him to her bedpost. It was kind of fun at first; Eddy was practically drooling from the fact that a female had given him the time of day, let alone taken her home for rutting.

He'd had women before, not his first time. Okay, only his second time. First time was when he was 28 when his father paid for him to visit a prostitute, figured it was time his son had some carnal experience. That had been a humiliation, for sure. His old man dropping him off at the local happy house in Kennel Town, so named for the pack of aging drug whores that prowled the streets. Yeah, old Dad left him with a wad of cash and went down to the bar below to get a beer. When Eddy came down 15 minutes later, his Dad had curled his lip at his poor performance and he endured the sneers and chortles of his Dad's crony buddies giving him the new nickname 'Fast Eddy'. Eddy endured. He always endured. He would show them all.

He lasted longer last night with his second conquest, for sure. But it was mostly because the skank had been into this bondage thing. She shouted at him after handcuffing him, telling him he was a worthless scumbag, and needed to show her the proper respect. Eddy didn't really get it, not what he had in mind, especially when she started whipping him with an old wet Barbie doll across his legs and chest.

Eddy whimpered from the pain and the humiliation and was thankful when she finally straddled his halfhearted hard-on. He grunted about 30 seconds later and again had to endure the curling lip of scorn. This time from a gutter whore. Fast Eddy became Faster Eddy. *He was done with them all.*

Eddy scrabbled his way to the elevator and then down to the bottom of the cavern. It was dark down there. Darkness made Eddy feel smaller, if that was possible. He sighed with relief as he switched on his flashlight and the world brightened a little. Eddy made his way deeper into the hole. On his back was a bag full of explosives. Eddy knew a little about them, had read about them as a teenager when he considered blowing up his school gym locker room to show all the jocks they couldn't hang him in a locker with a moldy cheese sandwich stuffed in his gym shorts. He'd chickened out, as usual. This time, however, he'd follow through, show all the big bastards.

Squaring his small shoulders Eddy made his way down and over to the scary statue, another big bastard, soon to become rubble. Eddy giggled as he took off his pack and set it to the ground. Eddy was completely creeped out by that gaze. He felt as if the eyes of the statue were watching him. It pissed him off, the judgment, the anger in them, just like his father. He picked up a rock and hurled it toward the nose. The rock careened off the chin taking a small satisfying chunk of it. "Fuck You!" Eddy screamed at the face. "Fuck YOU! Asshole!" Eddy started throwing more rocks, screaming at the top of his lungs, his reedy voice echoing heedless throughout the cavern. "Yeah, you like that you big fuck? Take that and that piss beard, I hate you, I fucking HATE YOU!" Eddy hurled the biggest rock he could at the face again with a scream born of years of frustration and humiliation "To hell with you!!!!!"

Tears formed in Eddie's eyes. Eddy wasn't a weeper. He hadn't actually really cried since fourth grade when the girl he loved scorned his advances and flicked a booger at his face. He buried his pain deep after that humilation and though he would sit at home and moan from time to time, he refused to cry. Now, he had had enough. He moved forward and began to smack at the base of the statue, heedless in his pain, of the rock ripping away at the skin on his hand. His tears began to flow, as did his blood. Finally, the physical and emotional pain was too much. He sat down in an emotional heap in front of the statue, his shoulders heaving with remorse over his loser life.

Nothing seemed to make sense anymore to Eddie, his life one chaotic cesspool of pain and disappointment. Waves of self-loathing poured out from him as he rocked back and forward in the dust. Eddie was oblivious to the fact that he had just opened a crack, a tiny fissure into another world with the power of his hatred and his pain. Eddie didn't know that his emotions had any power, beyond making him miserable, needing to be drowned in alcohol.

Eddy was wrong.

The energy waves absorbed through the stone and seeped through a tiny fracture from within; a tiny crack that opened a small opening into another world; a tiny crack that allowed a small part of something horrible to escape. Eddy didn't know any of this at that moment of course, he only knew, as he stared bleary-eyed and sobbing at the statue, that the eyes began to glow.

His yelp caught in his throat. His tongue waggled around like a piece of bologna as it tried to form the word 'help', or maybe it was 'Momma'. Rational thought fled along with yesterday's supper as the glow got brighter and Eddy's hold on his bowels disappeared.

The surface of the statue began to shimmer, and to Eddy's amazement, what looked like sweat appeared on the surface. The rock was becoming malleable; it was skin, real, alive, porous skin mixed with rock, twisting and fighting to maintain its hold in this world. The glowing eyes became more real, eyeballs rotating in their sockets seeming confused by their surroundings and the nose flaring and snorting heavy breaths as the statue struggled. A few moments longer of oozing transformation and Eddy was looking a giant living statue, roaming eyes, lips smacking paste, like a buried giant just waking up from a very long bender into the shit world of a severe hangover. The statue was still connected to the stone pedestal, as though it couldn't quite free itself.

Eddy also was frozen in place, but by fear. Soiled and trembling, he watched the statue wriggle in its rocky confines. He didn't know he was witnessing the partial release of an ancient prisoner, one who caused the death and destruction of his civilization, thousands of years before Eddy was whelped. Eddy didn't care about anything at that moment, he was praying he could be instantly transported anywhere right now; so terrifying was the creature before him. Anywhere, even back to the sneering sick broad with her wet Barbie Doll.

The giant eyes, glowing like barbecue coals, blinked several times as they took in their surroundings. They seemed to be gaining consciousness, and looking none too pleased at what they were seeing.

A thought finally began to seep into Eddy's skull. The one thought that had kept him alive all of his pathetic 34 years, kept him from getting beat up, spared him from his father's rages and his mother's death bed. 'RUN!' His legs finally caught up with his reason and he sprang to action. Too late. The eyes found him.

The eyes beheld Eddy's meager form, making him squirm. Then the light from the eyes intensified and

expanded outwards, surrounding him. A presence, an
essence of something or someone old and powerful, moved
around him, sizing him up, like a predator to its prey. Then,
without warning, the presence in the light entered Eddy,
plunged deep inside of him. Eddy felt like a hand was
reaching into his skull and grabbing his brain, like a wet
sponge from a bucket.

'RUN' thought turned to 'STRUGGLE' thought and
then to 'SCREAM' thought, but none of these thoughts
turned to action as Eddy had no control anymore over his
physical body. The terrible presence filled his mind, sifting
through his thoughts and memories like one would go
through a week-old sports section while sitting in the john.
It did not rush; the presence was patient, and thorough.

The deeper the presence went the further away Eddy's
hold on his sanity got. Terror was an abstract pleasure
compared to the intensity he felt. His heart was pounding as
he fought against the power and felt as though it would pop
through his chest.

Somewhere the thought came to Eddy that he was
about to die, his body could not tolerate any more. Eddie
sucked in a breath to try to scream when, abruptly, the fear
of his impending death disappeared in a flood of pleasure
that rolled exquisitely inside him for a moment. Then,
without warning, the pleasure vanished and Eddy felt
intense pain throughout his body, every fiber screaming in
agony, forcing Eddy to his knees. The pain went on
seemingly endless only to be replaced by joy, then soothing
reassurance. Pain, pleasure, pain, pleasure, back and forth
Eddy went between the extremes, the presence playing him
like a puppet from the inside. Waves of happiness lapped
over the shores of his intellect. He was in excruciating pain
one second, in love the next, at the point of climaxing the
next, as his tormenter learned the strings of its new Eddy
puppet. In the short while it had probed the depths of

Eddy's consciousness and his memories, and had learned all it needed about Eddy and his world.

Then came the voice, which filled Eddy's head, needful and soothing, a deep, sonorous rumble that shook Eddy's soul.

"I need you, Eddy. My place in this world is not complete. I need you. You want to help me don't you, Eddy?"

Pleasure. Eddy felt his head flap up and down. More pleasure came to Eddy at the thought of being needed and the desire within him to please a higher authority.

"You will be mine then, Eddy, and I will reward you."

Suddenly, images filled Eddy's head. Glorious images. Eddy as a king, cruising his empire city in a tricked out sweet ride. Entering his own club, VIP red carpet, strolling in with puffy-lipped, big-boobed babes all around him, wanting him, beckoning to him. He was the man. Men longed to be him, woman to have him. Some young muscled dude that looked remarkably like his father laughed at him as he walked in the front door of his club. With a flick of his finger the big bastard is taken out back and worked over by his boys as a naked woman rubs herself all over Eddie while refilling his glass. *Ooohhh yaaaa…*

"Stay with me, Eddy. That's a boy." Eddy was tugged gently back from his daydream by the voice.

Eddy snapped out of his dream, the images sadly fading away. "Who are you?" Eddy's voice sounded from a million miles away.

"I am Krynos. I can show you more. My history. My life. Then, you will understand. Do you want to see more, Eddy?"

Another wave of pleasure hit Eddy. Again, Eddy agreed.

To Eddy's surprise, the presence filled him more completely than it already had done already. Random images began to fill Eddy's head again. But this time more completely than before, like living memories, but not his own. Alien. The memories became more real, and even though Eddy knew they were taking place somewhere in his head and that his body was physically still in the cavern, the memories consumed him wholly, making him feel like he was actually there. He was Eddy and Krynos in one consciousness; Eddy/Krynos combined in his mind. Eddy found himself experiencing Krynos's past memories as though he was actually there in that time, as though he was Krynos, reliving his past in complete detail. It was weird. Good weird. Way better than the ecstasy he had taken once, way better. This was amazing. Eddy allowed himself to relax and let the memories take over.

Krynos's world was lush and green, beautiful beyond Eddy's comprehension. Earth as it should be. Unspoiled, vibrant, alive. A civilization existed here, advanced and shiny, but not in contrast to its natural surroundings. A city rose up in his mind: Ranton, a jewel in the sun. So seamlessly incorporated was it, that he could hardly tell where the buildings left off and nature started. Eddy knew immediately that there was no pollution, that renewable resources were harnessed to a degree that was god-like and unfathomable.

As he soared over the city, Eddie noticed that there were two kinds of people in this land, two races. The Delkar and the Mylogen. The Delkar were the newcomers. They had come to settle on the Earth many thousands of years after the Mylogen had first settled. The Delkars were welcomed with open arms and the two races lived peacefully, side by side, for many years. Krynos was a Delkar.

Eddy soared to a balcony top, high above the city, where two people, a man and a woman were locked in a passionate embrace, the edges of their bodies becoming one. In that intimate place, Eddy felt, for the first time in

his life, through Krynos's memory, love. Her name was
Mira. Eddy could see her in Krynos's memories, statuesque
and powerful with an extraordinary beauty that could move
men to tears. Their love was of the rarest kind, here in this
place of two races, for Mira was Mylogen.

The memories fast-forwarded in a strange flash, and
suddenly Krynos was soaring over a rugged mountain
range. How he was being transported was a mystery to
Eddie, but he felt no fear. Krynos loved to explore, loved
nature. The peace he felt as he drank in the fecund
landscape was overwhelming. He could stay here forever.
He loved the world. In that moment of pure bliss, a flash of
light caught his eye. Something sparkly and powerful was
beckoning to him. He could feel its presence in his mind,
warm, inviting.

Flash forward and Eddy was standing in a cave before
a glittering wall of jewels. Eddy thought they were jewels,
he shared Krynos' wonder at them, could feel the immense
power emanating from them. Krynos' excitement was also
Eddy's. The power was alluring and seductive. Krynos
could feel it reaching out to him. There was a pattern to the
jewels. About a thousand smaller gems arranged in a
circular pattern, surrounding three middle-sized stones
arranged at equidistance apart from each other.

At the center of the entire arrangement was a large
stone. This stone didn't glitter; it was dun coloured and
plain, yet Krynos could tell that this was the most powerful
of all. Eddy/Krynos reached out and placed a hand on the
stone. The stone became pliable and seemed to melt into
his hand. Krynos wanted to pull away, but found he could
not, and more, did not *want* to. The stone surrounded his
hand, and then became part of it. Pleasure and power oozed
up his arm and filled him inside and out.

Enshrouded in power Krynos became more than
himself, could see the possibilities of his power and it all
felt *soooo good.* He could bring good to his world. Move

them to new heights, cure the sick advance them beyond
anything they could imagine. This power was clearly a gift
of the creator, and Krynos was meant to bring it forth.

Eddy's vision fast-forwarded again. This time, Krynos
was standing before a great throng of people looking up to
him as he spoke of the glory of the power he had found, of
the great benefit for all. Krynos raised his transformed rock
hand and let them all behold the goodness. The crowd
cheered and swayed to the rocks power.

Another flash and Krynos was standing before the
council made up of representatives of Mylogen and Delkar,
votes being tallied, men and women standing in support of
him. Some not. Three among them, Guardians of the Earth,
held their seats, refused to rise along with their Mylogen
brethren. They argued that the power must be returned to
its place. Eddy felt Krynos's anger at their defiance; their
rejection of what was clearly good. It didn't matter;
Krynos would make them see, none would dare defy the
coming of good. With the power of the stone Krynos
swayed the Delkar to his cause, promising them all a
glorious future. The Delkars were easy to sway but the
Mylogens were somehow able to resist his power. Those
Mylogen that resisted Krynos fled, the three Guardians
among them.

Flash. Krynos waged a righteous war against the
Mylogen, he looked on them, with distrust and hatred.
These Mylogen were evil, they were the greatest resistance
to the good that Krynos offered. Krynos felt the satisfaction
as before the power of the stone they were rooted out by his
followers and died in horrible ways; they deserved it, they
were evil. They didn't understand.

Flash. Krynos felt betrayal. Eddy couldn't quite make
out the images Krynos was sending him at this point, so
clouded were they with emotions. Eddy saw Mira, her face
full of tears, saw a door opening and then could feel
Krynos' heart break.

Flash. Krynos stood alone in a chamber, the three defiant guardians who had fled, surrounding him. He would crush them. He raised his fist. They pulled back their long sleeves and in their hands they held the three stones that Krynos saw surrounding the center stone in the wall when they first discovered the stone of power. Krynos tried to lash out with the power but, to his surprise, was absorbed by the three. They moved closer in from all three sides. Krynos snarled and tried to unleash more power, could feel the determination of those that would stop him but could do nothing.

Krynos felt his body, destroyed, turn to stone, his life force drawn into a prison of a different dimension, trapped for all eternity.

Flash. The vision faded. Eddy returned to the cave and to himself.

Eddy's tears ran in rivulets down his pimply face. What a crime had been done to this Krynos, his own kind turning on him in their stupidity and their jealousy. Eddy felt convulsions of empathy wave through him. Strange, he'd never felt that way about another.

"That's right, Eddy." Krynos's sorrowful voice intoned. *"I was trapped by those who were evil. They scorned me when I tried to help. Now, after all these years, it is I who need the help."*

Eddy stood there in awe, that someone like this should need his help. "What is it I can do? I'm not powerful or don't even know much."

"I will give you power, Eddy, and knowledge. With your consent, I can work through you freely and we will help this world, create a new kingdom that will benefit all those who choose to follow."

Eddy felt a wave of power lick through his soul. He shuddered in delight. *Yeah, we'll smash all the big bastards who get in the way. And the girls will worship me.*

"Give me your consent now, Eddy."

From the back of Eddy's mind a tiny thought tried to push its way forward to Eddy.

Resist!

But Eddy was tired of being the loser, the underdog. He wanted to be the boss, the one to run the show, for once in his life. He pushed the thought ruthlessly away. Eddy made the decision right then and there and then felt a shift inside him as he gave his consent. Deep down, inside where his will resided. Eddy didn't even know it was there, or his to give away. But he did. There was a flash inside Eddy. Power, knowledge, and strength flowed through him. Eddy felt himself change in ways he could not even imagine. Eddy was reborn. Now he was a big bastard.

FOUR: A Ball of Nasty

A ball of nasty congregated in Trace's head cavity. He
was more hung-over than he could possibly imagine.
Dared not open his eyes. Not sure of what he might see,
because he wasn't quite sure where he was. Then a warm
arm flopped over his shoulder blades. He could hear a
female voice gurgle something sleepy and ill-formed.
Suddenly, the grappa night came back to him in a hazy
barrage of loud images. Seventeen shots in and the three
amigos were screaming with laughter as they fired walnuts
at Trace's head. Where the walnuts came from he hadn't a
clue, but they caused a nasty sting when they hit the
temple.

Trace had fired back. His ammo was dried lima beans,
far nastier when they connected but harder to aim,
especially in his fried state. At one point he went for an all
out assault, commando-raid style, hurling a handful at Sax
as he jumped for cover behind a couch. He ducked down
as Lima beans sailed over his head, right into the face of a
girl who was just coming in the door.

"What the hell? What are you jackasses doing? Hey
are those my friggin' dry stock!?"

The voice was deep and sultry with a stinging Latino
accent.

"Jesus,Sax I let you stay here, cause you are too stupid
to sign a lease, but you throw around my dried goods like
that?"

"Sorry Jen..." Sax had the decency to look sheepish.
Then cocked a sassy grin. "Want a drink, mi hermana
bella?"

"Shit Sax, you drank my Grappa too? Dad made that
for me, ass-wipe."

She took a short swig. Eyes swept to Trace. They tried to be cool but he could tell the subtle softening of appreciation. "Who's this asshole?"

Sax smiled and played the host. "This is Trace, my boss friend."

Jenn never took her eyes off Trace. She studied him like one would a mouth-watering dessert, deciding how it would taste and whether she would regret it afterward. She took a ridiculously long drink of grappa. Trace was waiting for a little choked gasp as her lips came off the bottle, but only a contented sigh rolled out. Then she smiled at him; a smile like the kind a snake gives to a mouse before they swallow them whole. Here was a lot of woman, curvy for days, almost cartoonish in roundness. Betty Boop on acid. Trace realized he faced an entire Latino sex-buffet and would be expected to devour the whole enchilada. He gulped at the challenge but was determined to succeed. She handed him the bottle a'la Eve to Adam. He took it and swallowed the poison thinking, *It's going to be a long night.*

So there Trace lay in the morning, paralyzed with hangover and having to pee with a near comatose Latino girl named Jen who had had him in ways last night he didn't know existed. Her breasts had filled his intoxicating vision as she had straddled him and ground him into orgasmic bliss. He sunk into her like a stone, plunging deep to escape the world as she rocked and moaned on his manhood in positions that he knew would haunt his muscles for days to come.

Later, panting, slick with sweat and spent, she threw him off her and passed out. But not before telling him in a sleepy, contented murmur that he could stay the night, but not to wake her in the morning when he left. *Wow. A good night, I guess. Certainly acrobatic.*

Somehow, though, in the pit of that place that couldn't be denied, he felt something he hadn't felt before. Regret?

Mild disgust? Boredom? His life felt like a disconnected set of random occurrences, without order, rhyme or reason. He was a million jigsaw pieces from many different puzzles, too confusing to bear. Trace took a deep breath. He knew that this road of morose mulling lead to nowhere, so he pushed the intrusive thoughts away with his will. He could bring them out later and roll over it in detail. *But later. Not now, later.* That is, if he survived the hangover. *Perhaps a little more sleep...*

In that moment, Trace's phone decided to start ringing. He moved as fast as he could over to his pants, which, for some reason, were tied in knots. Fishing out his phone, his head screaming and pounding, he managed to stumble out of the room with only the rebuke of a groan and a mumbled "Fuuuck" from Jenn, before he get out into the hallway and close the door. The phone continued to buzz. He answered. It was Agnes, her voice was pure and silky in contrast to the percussive grunge pit of Trace's hung-over morass.

Agnes's impatient tone chimed in. "Hello...you there?"

"Yeah, hey hi Agnes. What's doin'?

"You sound like a dying man, Mr. Anderson. I thought we were meeting this morning."

Trace searched wildly around him for an anchor to reality, shaking his head, willing his thoughts to order.

"Yep, for sure, 10am right?"

The sound like foot tapping entered her voice.

"Yes, well it's 11 o'clock Mr. Anderson, when can I expect you?"

"Sorry," Trace said, looking down at the wad of knotted pants. "I got a little tied up...with things. I can do Noon...maybe we can get some coffee..."

She cut him off from making a further ass of himself. "12 o'clock at the pit, Mr. Anderson, I can get my own coffee."

With that she hung up, leaving Trace bereft of the life raft of her angelic voice. Even angry, that voice resonated through him. Didn't know why...didn't have time to think about it. He shuffled off to the bathroom and managed to pull his shit together despite his kettledrum brain and was at the side of the pit looking at Agnes through the steam of her coffee at 11:59.

Trace was all smug about that one minute early and yet that disappeared quickly like her coffee steam when she casually commented "You look a little worse for wear, Mr. Anderson. That must have been some tying up."

Then she did a funny thing with a wistful smile that made him want her even more. It was like this knowing twitch with a hint of 'you will never know what I could do to you in the sack, pal'. Like she was in this elite club of deliciousness that only a rarified few get to explore. Not guys like Trace. But man, did he ever want in that club, though he knew that he could only drool at its locked membership doors. *Shit.*

Agnes's mysterious smile disappeared, replaced by her no-nonsense, serious face and she whirled away, leaving him gangling along in her wake. They hit the ladder and made their way to the bottom in silence. As the two worked their way over to old bug eyes' statue, they both noticed at once that something was wrong.

The statue had a big chunk missing from the chin. The face too is somehow different. The mouth, which was a snarling mess before, now seemed to grin with satisfied pleasure.

"How the hell? Okay I know I'm a little worse for wear, but wasn't that face different yesterday?"

Agnes began to answer, then stopped as she heard footsteps crunching from behind. Trace whirled around, the movement causing his brain to flutter with pain. Standing before him was a short, slight man in an immaculate black suit.

"What the....? How'd you get down here? Who are you?" Trace demanded of the small man.

"Allow me to introduce myself." He said.

His voice was benign and cultured, speaking in English peppered with several accents, like he learned different words of the English language in a dozen different countries.

"I am Mr. Noth. I am sorry to intrude and startle you both.

"Trace turned to Agnes, "You know this guy?"

She ignored Trace and answered by stepping over to Mr. Noth and extending her luscious hand.

"I'm Agnes, department of Archeology." Her voice was too soothing for this odd situation.

Trace decided he could also act formally and business-like. "I'm Trace..."

Before he can finish, however, Mr. Noth smoothly cut in. "Yes Mr. Anderson. I believe you are responsible for this location."

"How did you know who I am?"

"It is my need and my interest to know such things Mr. Anderson."

He held his hand out to Trace. His hand was warm and firm, not what Trace expected. Noth held on to his hand a little longer than etiquette dictated and Trace was about to jerk his hand back when suddenly, he felt something pass between them. A small surge of energy moved from Noth's hand to Trace's and then distributed itself throughout his body. Trace felt his body rejuvenate from Noth's touch, like getting a shower and a spa treatment from the inside. A little creepy, but sure cleared his hung-over besotted head, way better than coffee.

"What the hell...?" Trace began to protest or thank or question or something. *What the hell just happened?*

Agnes looked confused at the exchange and the look of surprised bewilderment on Trace's face. Before he could get his mouth to comment on the whole weird moment, Noth released Trace's hand and waved dismissively as he walked away from the two over to the statue.

"I need you clear headed for this Mr. Anderson." Noth said.

Finally Trace's mouth spats out his confusion. "Wait a minute who are you?" he asked. "Did Janks..."

"Your company doesn't even know I exist, Mr. Anderson," Noth answered. "Few people do. But you have need of me, both of you. And so does this world."

Before Trace could burp out a response, Agnes piped in, perplexed.

"Please tell me what you mean, Mr Noth? Do you know about this statue? Are you from an institution, university.... research team?"

Trace looked again at Noth's suit, thinking he looked like he came out of a funeral home in the 1800s. Noth started to speak again.

"This statue was buried thousands of years ago by the first civilization to live on its cultured surface. The Mylogens were planet farmers and pioneers, like your early American Settlers. The Mylogens existed from before the universe reset itself and colonized the galaxy. Earth was one of them. They came to this world more advanced than you could conceive. They settled a civilization here and lived in peace for 500,000 years. Can you imagine such a thing, Mr. Anderson? 500,000 years of peaceful existence."

Trace glanced at Agnes; her stunned look looked stunning on her, but was still stunned. She looked back at Trace for a moment and he had the feeling she thought he was pulling some enormous prank on her. Trace looked as innocent and possible smiling his best boy smile at her.

She turned back to Noth. "Mr. Noth. I'm not sure where you get your fantasies from, but there is no evidence of any civilization this advanced known to have existed..."

Unruffled, Noth smoothly stopped her with a raised hand. "This is no fantasy, I assure you..."

Agnes cut in, clearly not liking the hand, "I have studied Archaeology a long time, and I'm also a fan of fantasy fiction..."

Trace's head watched the tennis match between the two, *nothing like smart people first thing in the morning.*

Noth's mellifluous voice soothed her ruffled feathers. "I know the question you are thinking, Miss Argwhistle, 'why is this the only evidence'," his head nodded in the direction of the statue, "Because when the Mylogens leave a planet, they till the soil and return it to its natural state...This time, however, things were different. They had to leave him behind."

Noth walked over to the statue and looked up at its menacing eyes as though it were alive and could hear him.

"They had to imprison him here because moving him would be too risky. So they locked him away and left the chaos behind."

Trace was more than baffled. Even refreshed by the magic handshake or whatever the hell that was, this tale was pushing his brain to its capacity. He chimed in, trying to keep the conversation straight.

"Okay, let's get back to the happy monster statue here."

"Allow me to continue" Noth said.

Trace waved his hand in surrender. Clearly, Noth had a story to tell and wasn't going to be side-tracked from it. Trace looked over at Agnes, who shrugged soft shoulders that he really wanted to touch. He turned back to Noth.

"The floor is yours"

Noth bowed his head.

"The Mylogens came to this planet and created a vast civilization in this area of your world, it's capital was Ranton, a sparkling jewel of a city, the crowning achievement of the settlers. They governed as equals, everyone sharing in the responsibilities of their beloved world. After a time, around 300,000 years after the Mylogens cultivated Earth, another race known as the Delkar, came to Earth and decided they would also like to settle on this planet. The Mylogens, being peaceful, had no problem sharing and welcomed them openly. They co-existed for thousands of years. One day, only a few thousand years ago, a bright young Delkar, named Krynos, came across that which must not be touched; an energy Sourcestone hitherto unknown in all of the cultured worlds, unique to Earth. The Sourcestone contained a rogue energy dimension, a fluke of its creation, contained within a small rock. Where it came from, nobody was sure. The Mylogens called it Cha-sos...you know it today as chaos."

"The original Mylogens, those who first cultivated the earth had, discovered it and surrounded it with powerful wards known as Keystones in order to minimize its influence and keep those who would meddle with it away. They could not destroy it, for it was native to this world and they sensed it was intrinsically tied to its well being, how, they were not sure. The Mylogens always worked within the boundaries of the nature of a world, they did not try to destroy and remake in their image as your kind do."

At this, Noth glanced around at the machinery and scaffolding within the cavern, then back at Trace, his pointed look making him squirm.

"The Sourcestone remained in stasis until Krynos discovered it, by accident, hundreds of thousands of years after Earth was first colonized by the Mylogens. How he managed to release it from the protection of its Keystones, I am not sure. He found it and the energy of Chaos seduced him, twisted him, making him believe he could use the power for the good of both our races. Krynos discovered that he could control the Delkar through the power of the Sourcestone, by influencing their wills and making them do his bidding."

"Did the Mylogens also fall under Krynos's spell?" Agnes asked.

"A good question. Somehow, the Mylogens were immune to the power and they resisted, but it was too late. Krynos twisted what was once a peaceful co-existence into something horrible. He hunted the Mylogens and would have brought them to their knees had he not been betrayed by someone very close to him."

"Who betrayed him?" Trace asked.

"His mate, Nerina. Someone who he loved very much."

"But why wasn't she under Krynos's control?"

"Because Nerina was a Mylogen."

Trace let out a low whistle. "You mean she betrayed her people…"

"…for the man she loved." Noth finished. "Yes, in the beginning she wanted to believe him and thought he was only trying to do good. But when Krynos began to hunt the Mylogen, it was too much for her and she betrayed him."

"This betrayal gave the break the Mylogen needed to subdue Krynos and bring him down. His mind control became more erratic and unstable and he lost control over the power and soon the entire civilization was plunged into chaos. It was only the efforts of a few who held out before him, after much grief and loss, that he was defeated. Using the keystones they were able to re-contain the energy back in its rightful place, but in so doing imprison Krynos's essence with it. Krynos's body was destroyed, turned to the statue you see before you. It was buried here when they left, for they dared not destroy it lest they allow Chaos to be released unchecked again in your world. After that, the

Mylogens gathered up their kind and forced the Delkar to leave with them."

The effort of trying to absorb Noth's speech, was making Trace's head return to the state of an out of balance washing machine in spin mode. *Where did this guy come from?* In the intervening silence Trace looked at the serious face of Noth, then burst out laughing. *This is ridiculous! Am I now in a post-curvy-Latino and grappa hallucination?*

Trace chuckled from the depths of his being and looked to Agnes to enable him in his mirth. *Wrong move.* She stood all gog-eyed at the self-proclaimed alien. *What the hell? Is this her type? Where can I get a suit like that? Museum? Film set costume truck? Madame Tusades?* There seemed to be no winning bones being thrown to his bruised cerebellum this morning. He decide to play along. He choked back his laughter and tried to look as serious as the other two.

Agnes ignored him and turned to Noth. "Mr. Noth. If what you say is true, about these Mylogens leaving the planet and destroying all evidence of their being here, who or what are you?"

Trace opened his mouth to respond, but before a witty retort could drip off his sock-thick tongue, however, Noth started again. "They couldn't leave things completely alone, Ms. Argwhistle, may I call you Agnes?"

Yeah even an alien could see the mirth in that name, Trace thought.

Agnes acquiesced with a nod of her head as Noth continued.

"After Ranton was erased from the Earth, some Delkar, not wanting to be forced to leave by the Mylogens, escaped and hid, eventually allowing themselves to be absorbed into your race. The Mylogens did not believe in this kind of intermingling, but saw their role as caretakers instead. They watched the earth, sent periodic scouts to report on what they found. As the millennia passed and human beings began to propagate and dominate, they made contact. Of course those first attempts were disconcerting, the 'locals' were too apt to look upon the Mylogens as Gods. They could not form an effective watch force. They also did not wish to contaminate the natural development of the human race as the Delkar had done and so they sent scouts to blend in."

Trace piped into the narrative at this point.

"Like spies, James Bond, and all that?" He turned to Agnes. "How about that? Mrs. Moneypenny?" He had given Agnes his best Sean Connery, but was met with four stony eyes, not amused by the big hung-over clown.

Noth pressed on, unperturbed.

"Those scouts joined society as needed and monitored the situation. For thousands of years, they kept watch. Until war overtook their own kind in another part of the galaxy and they were forced to go home to join the resistance. We have only just returned. Too late it seems."

"Did he say, we?" Trace's scalp began to get all tingly. "WE? Okay, so...your now telling us that you are a Mylogen? A Mylogen in a formal suit come back to check on your statue? Wow, really Agnes, you can't be buying this load of..."

Agnes cut him off by walking over to the statue.

"What do the words mean?" Agnes nodded toward the inscriptions hammered out on it.

Noth joined Agnes and ran his little hand across them. *At least the Mylogens were little, if Noth was any indication.* Trace thought. *If it came down to a fight, this guy would go over in a strong wind.*

A cloud of sadness fell over Noth's face as he read the words.

"In remembrance of that which is not allowed to be. Be vigilant. Be strong. Look to your future and be steadfast in your duty"

Tears stood out in Noth's eyes. For a moment the little
man seemed a lot more than what he presented. Trace's
vision wavered for a moment and Noth's bearing and face
changed. At once, he seemed immensely old to Trace and,
re-evaluating his diminutive stature in an instant,
immensely powerful. Then the vision was gone as fast as
He'd seen it, Noth returned to tweedy insignificance. But
Trace had seen it, there was no denying it, it was not a trick
of his hangover. And the image of Noth had made its
impression on him and he was mute in his desire for mirth
and deflection. Agnes had seen also, Trace could see it in
her eyes, a kind of fascinated horror slid into place on her
face. She spoke up quietly, not wanting to intrude with her
voice, it seemed, on a personal moment.

"Why too late?" She asked.

Noth turned to both of them, his face grave. "Last
night one of your kind came here and allowed a part of
Krynos's essence to escape."

"What are you talking about?" Trace asked. The tone
in Noth's voice had sent chills through his body.

"There is a crack into the world of chaos, a tiny
hairline crack, through which Krynos has managed to
worm a part of his being into this world. He's looking for
the Keystones of course. Once he was imprisoned, the keys
were removed to a safe place. Krynos has sent his essence
forth to find the keys. Once his prison is fully opened, he
will be able to extend his influence on the world
completely, with unlimited access to the power of Chaos.
He will carry on with his original quest, to unleash chaos
upon the world. The power of chaos has fully bent Krynos
to do its bidding, an energy he has been intimate with for
thousands of years, an energy that he thinks he can control,
to create his idea of good. He will be unstoppable."

Trace's head pain had returned. He looked at Agnes
who seemed to be buying all of what Noth was selling,
hook, line and sinker. He was still skeptical, despite all that

he experienced today. Trace knew he had his dreamer side; he got that from his mother. But his Dad was a no-nonsense military man and that part of him was asserting itself.

"Okay, let's not get all Gollum on us okay Noth? Maybe your an elf or something, but I assure you that this is not the crack of doom, fella. Or a shire..."

Trace started to rant then, but before he could continue however, the Noth started to glow.

A soft halo appeared around his whole body, the light spreading out to cover both Agnes and Trace and the entire cavern. Then the world of the Cavern shifted and changed, reconstituted to what it had been so long ago. In a few moments their world had disappeared entirely.

They stood in a chamber of light. Dazzling beyond comprehension, bejeweled and polished; designed as a thing of beauty. In the center of the chamber stood a tall young man, his face twisted in defiant horror at those who confronted him. Three robed figures surrounded him in an equilateral triangle. In the crook of their left arms they held a shining colored stone, one blue, one yellow, and one red. The colors were reaching out towards Krynos, intermingling into a rainbow at the center of the triangle, surrounding him.

The three robed figures held their ground, as Krynos raised his hands and lightning and pure destructive energy poured from his fingertips, only to be absorbed by the colours. Those wielding it didn't have an easy time of it. Clearly the stones were linked to them and it was only through a battle of wills that they held their ground, absorbing the energy as they did. The colours coalesced into a triangular black box, surrounding Krynos on all sides.

Trace couldn't believe what he was seeing. The black pyramidal box closed in around Krynos and became one with him, deforming his form as it struggled within its new found prison. The energy increased as Krynos's struggles

began to ebb and transform. Trace was transfixed as the
energy creature that was Krynos began to turn to stone.
Within a few moments all of Krynos had been transformed
into the giant rock statue he saw before him.

The energy subsided and the three holding the
keystones walked away in the direction they had come. The
scene then faded. The brilliance transformed once again
into the cavern in which the three stood. Trace looked over
at Agnes. Her delicious mouth was parted in awe. Trace
knew his mouth was hanging open also but imagined he
looked more like a dog seeing a giant can of food. Noth
seemed a little drained by what he had just conjured.
Drained and sad.

It was Agnes who spoke first. "Your home?" Noth
nodded.

"What?! You mean you're one of those dudes with the
stones?" Trace said.

Noth nodded again and Trace's stomach dropped. He
forced the feeling down. He was not about to bring up his
previous evening with his Latino goddess in front of
Agnes; instead, he plopped down on a nearby boulder.

*Wow, a guy got turned to stone right where I was
sitting. WEIRD.* Trace had had a few mushroom induced
hallucinations in his time but nothing compared to this. He
was a skeptic, for many things, but this seemed too bizarre
not to be real.

Trace looked over at Agnes. Her big eyes met his,
filled with concern and fear. He could tell from her look
that she was a believer, which surprised him, as she didn't
strike Trace as the type to do things against her beautiful,
logical nature. She half-smiled at him, and for Trace that
meant his cup was half-full. For some reason, it made him
feel good, just looking at her. *Her energy or something.*
There was something he'd never felt before. *A flutter.
What? What was that? Come-on Trace, You're not in*

grade six again playing footsy in science class with Kathy Salter. Pull it together.

Yet somehow, Trace knew something had shifted in him. Not something he was going to think about immediately. Yet he knew as he looked at Agnes, he wanted to protect her and keep her safe. He also wanted to poke fun at her and laugh at her inconsistencies. But that's what boys do to girls, after they graduate from punching them in the arm. It was surprising when Trace spoke up, knowing he had made a decision not to run away. This Noth guy needed something from them and Trace knew, regardless of the craziness of it all, they were going to help him.

"So what do you mean about this energy, Krynos thing? How do you know somebody helped him?"

Noth looked at Trace and nodded approval. "For that, Mr. Anderson we need to see your security cameras."

Half an hour later the three were sitting in front of a screen divided into quadrants, kind of like the show Hollywood squares Trace used to watch as a kid. Except in each quadrant was a fixed camera shot of a part of the construction site, rather than some has-been actor ready to doll out droll witticisms and sarcastic observations. Trace pushed a button on the keyboard and the camera square covering the cavern went black for a second as a clock scrolled time back. *It sure would be cool to have one of these on your life.* Trace thought. *Just scroll back to a cool event like the first time you won a soccer game, or got laid, very awesome.*

As they watched the screen, the evening sunlight disappeared from the entrance of the cavern; the night-lights popped on, illuminating the cave with long shadows. At about 10:30pm a figure passed through the opening and walked toward the statue. Even from the low light and fuzzy video Trace knew who this was. He'd been in and about the site since work started. A little ferret kind of guy who could never look at one spot for long, always licking his lips and seemingly uncomfortable in his own skin.

Trace groaned. Noth and Agnes looked up at him.

"Do you know this man?" Noth asked.

"Yeah I know him, unfortunately. His name's Eddy. Does grunge work for Chuck Layton. Errand boy, piss collector. Has a nasty side to him also." Trace remembered one day Eddy came around demanding some paperwork for Chuck. When he told Eddy it wouldn't be ready until the following day, the guy actually snarled and bared his teeth at him. "If he's involved, it's not good."

Agnes, Noth and Trace watched Eddy's pathetic rock throwing, and then his meltdown as he tried in vain to beat up the statue with his bare hands. Then the statue's eyes started to glow.

"What is THAT?!" Trace asked.

"That is Krynos. A part of him has been released."

"What?" Trace asked. "How did that happen? A dozen people have been down there since the cave-in. How is it that that little shit Eddy Smiter released this creep Krynos?"

"There are two things at play here. Firstly, Earthlings have a similar genetic makeup to the Delkar. They do not have the Mylogen resistance to the power of Chaos inherent within them." Noth looked again at Eddy on the screen. "The difference between Eddy and the others that have been down here is his emotional state and the waves of energy his anger and distress are giving off. Most humans are unaware of the energies they give off."

Noth paused looking from Agnes to Trace, before speaking again. "Humans don't even realize how much they affect one another. Two strangers sitting side by side, never speaking, have shared energies that are profound without ever knowing."

In that moment Trace could feel the heat beginning to rise within him as he became consciously aware of Agnes's presence beside him. Agnes shifted her position in her chair without ever looking away from Noth, then, after a moment she cleared her throat and brought the conversation back to the video.

"So how did this energy from Eddy help Krynos?"

Noth smiled for a moment as he regarded her, then continued.

"Krynos, it seems, has been working from the inside to erode a his prison. It would appear that he was somehow able to seize on Eddy's energy to open a small crack to escape a part of his essence into this world."

Trace was beyond skeptical.

"That's quite the leap don't you think, Noth? I mean, assuming for the moment that we are not all crazy and this is some strange hallucination, what are the odds of something like this happening? Seems all pretty far-fetched...am I being punked right now?"

"No Mr. Anderson. I assure you there is no 'punking' going on. I wish I could offer you some solace in a seemingly uncontrived scenario, but unfortunately this is the way things seem to work. Remember, Krynos is imprisoned in Chaos, a place where rules and logic do not apply. Humans seem to depend on the randomness of this energy to advance forward through time, their lives are a continual struggle to bring order to chaos. Order is the antithesis of Chaos, the Keystones work through this principal. But Krynos has recreated some of the rules that imprison him. So yes, Eddy's emotional state was just thing he needed in order to free a part of himself."

Distracted by movement on the screen Trace sat forward squinting at the screen. The eyes in the statue had stopped glowing. There was a halo of light swarming around Eddy. "What the hell is going on?"

Noth leaned into the screen. "He is being sifted by Krynos's energy."

Trace and Agnes looked confused. "Sifting him? Like flour? What do you mean?" Asked Agnes.

"No, Mylogen and Delkar are selective telepaths. We can read the thoughts of others, but only by invitation. To do so without invitation is comparable to mental rape. Krynos, with the power of Chaos, can manipulate the psychological and physical experiences of his victims through their similar genetic link, but in order to inhabit his victim totally and work through them to forge a link to others, his victim must agree. He must willingly agree to being overtaken."

On the screen, they watched Eddy fall to the ground clutching his head as he was 'sifted', his body going limp and lifeless. Then after about twenty minutes, he sprang to life again, jumping to his feet with an athletic grace.

"I guess Eddy gave his permission, there's no way that dweeb could move like that."

"Precisely Mr. Anderson."

On the screen, Eddy disappeared out of the Cavern, shouldering his pack as he left. What was in that pack, Trace could only guess, but he was sure it had something to do with Chuck's earlier request to blow up the cavern.

"What's he going to do now, Mr. Noth?" Agnes asked. "Where will he go?"

"Krynos wants those keys. He will pour his energy and his resources into finding them."

"Does he know where they are?" Agnes asked.

"No, not exactly. He can sense them for they are linked to the statue after all. When they were removed, they left a thread of energy. "

"Like Hansel and Gretel and the bread crumbs?" Trace said.

"Precisely, Mr. Anderson. But I have hidden the trail well and masked the location as best as possible. He will want those keys to open the door to his prison. He will stop at nothing in order to achieve his goal."

"Yeah, but who's going to help that sorry excuse for air?" He said pointing at the screen and the now frozen image of Eddy.

"Krynos can divide his energy and enter other willing hosts. He does so like forging a chain. This 'Eddy' is the first chain in the link. If a chain in the link is broken, all the links after it will be broken. Furthermore, each subsequent link weakens his essence, but only by a small amount. He can't raise an army at this point, even if there are millions of genetically compatible hosts. But, I suspect he can raise a small enough team to help him complete the task. If his task is completed, Earth as we know it will cease to exist. Chaos will reign...everywhere."

<><>

"Okay." Trace said as they came out of the security trailer walking toward the parking lot where Agnes is parked. "So why are you telling us?" He looked at Agnes but her expression was unreadable. "Why don't you just call your boys down from planet wherever and wrap this guy up again?"

Clearly that was the wrong thing to say. Trace didn't think it could be possible for anyone to look sadder than Noth did at that moment. Agnes shot Trace a perfectly manicured, non-plussed eyebrow. "What? What did I say?" He looked at Noth. "What did I say to make you the poster boy for defeat?"

Noth took a moment to answer. When he did, his voice seemed very tired and far away. "Well, Mr. Anderson, the problem I lost contact with them some time ago. I have not heard from them since."

"I? I thought you implied there were more Mylogens who first scouted the" humans?" Agnes said.

"I'm afraid I mislead you somewhat there, Agnes. Only one scout was sent as watcher to the early humans. Resources were scarce you see, since our war, and there was little personnel to spare."

"It was you...?" Trace's synapses weren't quite able to mentally digest this newest piece of information.

Noth looked at both of them and slowly nodded.

"Okay, you said your kind is long lived...How long since you lost contact are we talking here, Mr. Noth?" Trace asked, knowing the answer was going to be disturbingly impressive.

"5000 years. About a thousand years after I arrived."

Trace blew out an incredulous breath. "Sweet mother of all that is grungy and fucked up. Are you serious? You mean to tell me you're 5000 years old?"

Noth smiled a little at that notion, apparently hiding their age was a vanity thing among Mylogens. "Holding steady at 4999? Is that the deal Noth?"

Noth actually chuckled at the notion of his vanity. "Actually, Mr. Anderson, I'm a 15432 Earth years old...next week"

Trace felt his knees go weak and let out a low whistle and even Agnes had the decency to look a little beatifically discomfited.

Trace stopped walking and turned to her. "You know Agnes, It is a little surprising to me that I'm buying all this. But I am."

She took a long time to answer. "I am too, Mr. Anderson" She turned to Noth. "Alright, Mr. Noth, what do we do now? Go after this Eddy person?"

"That would be far too dangerous, Agnes. No, I need you two to locate and secure the Keystones. That will be dangerous enough."

Warning bells went off in Trace's head. "How come I get the impression that this is going to be far from simple? Can't you just beam the keystones here?"

"Unfortunately my influence is very limited. I will help when I can, but without me, there is no hope of resealing the prison." He looks at both of us, a gentle, encouraging smile appearing on his face. "This will be difficult, but not impossible."

"Why don't you just go to the government, top secret stuff and all that?" I asked. "Get some spies and FBI dudes with cool gadgets and stuff?"

"You are an interesting boy/man aren't you Mr. Anderson? Unfortunately, we will get no timely help from the authorities. They would probably lock us all away."

"And suck out your brain, eh Noth." Trace said.

"Precisely."

Agnes moved over to Trace's side, looking scared but determined. There was heat coming off of her and she was breathing hard. Somehow, since Noth had mentioned it, Trace seemed more aware of Agnes, as a human, a person, and not just a destination for his own desires. It was strange and different for Trace, who had always been caught up in his own agenda, his own energy. For the first time in his life, he really saw another person as a separate entity with their own energy, but somehow affecting his own. He smiled at her then, trying to make her feel at ease.

"You up for this Miss Argwhistle? Want to have an adventure?"

Something in the tone of Trace's voice made her look for a moment differently at Trace, then she simply nodded and shrugged. "Do we have another choice?"

FIVE: Bad Guys

Harry Barniker wanted to screw himself; if Harry Barniker could have cloned himself, but as a woman, he'd have his perfect life partner. When Harry looked in the mirror, he imagined himself screwing himself. Perfection. Harry saw blonde curly hair, a strong jaw, perfect skin and teeth-an Adonis head on a better than Adonis body complete with abs to make the ladies melt.

The rest of the world viewed the reflection differently, however. Shaggy dark blond hair dripping down to narrow set eyes, a Neanderthal jaw with over-sized-ready-to-eat-raw-meat teeth, a body that was clearly jumped up on steroids, blocky and impressive in it's meanness and intrusion into space. His posture was that of someone who worked out too much, hulking and scary.

That's why the rest of the world kept their mouth shut around Harry. He wasn't afraid to use his steroid bulk to intimidate and bully. That's how Harry made his fortune-he cracked skulls on his way up the ladder, and when he got rich enough, he hired others to crack skulls for him. But Harry didn't see any of that in his reflection; he saw only perfection and strength (and virility). When Eddy Smiter strolled unannounced into his office interrupting his reverie, his self lust turned to rage, as it did so often.

"Who the fuck are you?" Harry stared down at the little spit in front of him; at what he considered the antithesis of himself. "And how the fuck did you get in here?"

He took a menacing step toward Eddy. Usually this was the only move he needed and was surprised when the little shit wipe in front of him didn't budge. Harry stopped and stared into the little man's eyes. What he saw there made him feel something he hadn't felt since his father punched him in the jaw when he was ten for breaking his favourite coffee cup. Fear. An odd sensation for Harry, to be sure.

Eddy simply looked the big guy over from head to toe like he was dissecting him, making Harry feel even more afraid. "I let myself in, Mr. Barniker. Your secretary was most accommodating."

Harry wasn't quite sure what that meant but didn't like the implication in Eddy's sneer. When Harry spoke again his voice was surprisingly deferential. He felt somehow as though he was speaking to a superior, another new sensation for Harry.

"What is you want here? Who are you?"

Eddy didn't miss the change in Harry's tone and smiled inwardly at how fast the big bastard had changed his tone. "I have a proposition for you that I know you can't refuse..."

Half an hour later Harry was a puddle of brain mush. Working through Eddy, Krynos had gone to work on Harry, although it took a bit longer on Harry. Promises of fame and fortune and power didn't really hold much interest to a man who was already quite powerful. Krynos abandoned what he usually offered, then went to work on why Harry was the way he was. Why did a human need to take steroids and bulk himself up into a monstrous body?

After much sifting, Krynos finally found the reason behind the wall of muscles. He had to go back very far in Harry's youth to find it. When he was six Harry loved to draw, had done so since he was even younger, his mother encouraging him with endless art supplies, brushes and paint and paper, Harry loved it and he loved his mother intensely. Then tragedy struck and Harry's mother was taken away from him, ripped away by the sudden swerving of an oncoming car. Harry had been in the car and heard his mothers final scream, a scream that still woke him, bathed in sweat, in the middle of the night.

Harry was then removed from his heaven on earth and forced to go live with his abusive father his mother had left years before. Ned Barniker was beyond mean, he was cruel. He set about a campaign to strip Harry of his softness, brainwash him, reprogram to be hard like him. When Harry was twelve, he took his first swing at his father and was beaten to a pulp for it, and then locked in a room for a week and told he would not be allowed out until he was harder and tougher. In that room, during that week, Harry made some choices and when he emerged a week later he was exactly what his father had wanted him to be. Harder and tougher.

It would take three years of constant weightlifting and martial arts to get to the point to be able to show his father how well his campaign to toughen Harry had been. By the time he was sixteen he stood over his father's beaten and bloody body proving to him how much harder and tougher he had become.

Krynos sifted through this sad tale and found Harry's weakness. Krynos brought the memory of his mother back to Harry, in full detail as though she were actually with Harry the adult. Harry's walls began to crumble, he wept a river of tears at the enveloping feel of his mother, brought back from a long lost locked box within him. Harry didn't know that Krynos could not actually bring back the dead; he was too wrapped up in the feeling of the arms that used to encircle him and keep him safe from harm. Then Krynos made the feeling go away and Harry wept harder at reliving the loss all over again as he had done at eight. Harry was lost in the chaos of his own feelings and pleaded to Krynos to bring his mother back. With her, life had made sense, since her loss, Harry had felt adrift on a sea of senseless random anger.

Krynos brought back the promise of Harry's mother to him, as though he was looking at her from a distance, just out of reach. He could see her, yearn for her, but only if he did exactly what Krynos wanted could he be able to reach her.

Now, Harry was completely in Krynos's control. It had felt so good to Eddy to watch Harry squirm and give in to what Krynos had offered so reasonably. Eddy felt like the big bastard now, and he had to admit he liked it. Little-big fucker. "Okay Harry Let's see our prison."

Harry smiled benignly. It felt good to want to do another's bidding, another new sensation for him. If he did good his mother would be returned. He would be the good boy his Mommy wanted.

"What do you want me to do?" Harry asked.

"I need to monitor the pit. Can you do that from here? Oh, and call me sir."

Harry nodded eagerly. "Yes, yes I can. I have a direct feed to the pit from here. That way I can keep an eye the progress."

"Like to be in control don't you, Harry?"

"Yes sir."

"Feels good to order people around?"

"Yes sir."

Eddy leaned over the desk, raised his hand and backhanded Harry across the face. The big man barely flinched. Inside, Harry he knew he should be outraged at the assault, would have killed for such an act. Now, though...he felt sorrowful and wondered what he had done wrong.

Harry's sad face made Eddy burst out laughing.

"That's right you big fuck. I'm the boss now...got it? Huh?"

Eddy raised his hand for another blow when Krynos's voice inside his head rang out causing him to flinch from pain. *"Get on with this...we have no time for your indulgences!"* Inwardly, Eddy whimpered. *"And remember...you are also dispensable."*

Eddy nodded to himself and for a neurotic moment wondered if Harry could hear that exchange. The big man's face, however, remained sorrowful and passive.

"Punch up the security tapes for the last 24 hours." Eddy came around to Harry's side of the desk and ordered him to stand in the corner. Sitting in the big man's chair he began sifting through the footage...not sure what he was looking for.

Krynos's voice in his head began again. *"I sensed an energy there since you freed my essence. An old presence almost forgotten....THERE!"*

Krynos's scream in his head almost dropped Eddy out of the chair to the floor. The voice gentled *"Hold there."* On the screen a frozen image of a small compact man in a business suit. *"That one"*

"Who is he?" Eddy squeaked, still smarting from the blow to the inside of his head. "Looks like an accountant."

Krynos's voice reverberated though his skull. *"He is our enemy, Eddy."* Suddenly Eddy felt a soothing touch on his nervous system, a gentle massage on the inside of his body. In a moment it was gone, leaving Eddy wanting.

"Who are those other two on the screen, Eddy?"

Eddy looked at the screen, a beautiful red-head was talking to the big asshole Trace. She was a beauty, nice ripe body. Eddy felt his hear rate go up at the thought of her, his breathing quickened. "The broad is the architect I heard about from Chuck Veeman told me about. And the big fuck is Trace Anderson. Big dumb loser overseeing excavation." His eyes drifted back to Agnes sliding down her body, imagining.

"You find her appealing, Eddy?"

Eddy swallowed. "Yes."

"Then she is yours. You may have her, and then you may kill her. Both of them."

For a moment Eddy felt his lust intensify, then at the mention of killing he felt his soul recoil. For a moment Krynos's presence faded. Eddy felt like he was coming out of a dream, but only for a moment, then Krynos presence filled his mind like never before soothing, compelling, alluring. Eddy could feel drool sliding out of his mouth. His breath coming in ragged heaves. *"Such things must be done, Eddy, for the good of all. THESE people would destroy us, they are evil, and they deserved punishment. Would you see the world suffer because of you weakness?"*

The word weak echoed throughout his brain in the voice of his father. Eddy felt anger welling up in his chest, hands clenched to fists. He felt power course through his body, he wanted to smash, to destroy to conquer. He wanted the world to know that Eddy Smiter was not weak. He would show them all.

"Fuck 'em, let's kill them all."

Laughter filled his mind. *"Good! Good, Eddy. But patience, one at a time. We don't want to over extend ourselves."* Eddy looked at Noth. *"No Eddy, not him. Him you can leave to me. Now let's see about some more recruits...I need you to help me enlist some help. The same way we did with Harry here. Me through you. We'll form a chain of men that will do our bidding."*

Eddy beamed with pride as the image of him commanding men appeared in his head. He, Eddy Smiter a general! A great man. If only his father had lived to see him now. If only...

The voice brought him back from his reverie.
"Time to plan Eddy. Time to win."

SIX: First Date

Trace shuffled his way toward Tank, after seeing off Noth and Agnes, his head full of the day. A crazy person would have thought he was crazy. Ancient civilizations. Ancient beings. Well-educated, beautiful women. Sounded like a trashy novel, the kind you killed hours over at a beach. He creaked the door open, went inside and retrieved a beer from the fridge.

Slumping his tired body down on his bed, Trace's thoughts roamed towards Agnes. Just what was it that caused his compass to steer in her direction? Even now, with the fantastical facts swimming around his brain, first and foremost was Agnes; like a figurehead on the boat of his crazy life. *Wow.* He'd never had this experience before. Well once, in grade 12 when Carolyn Dobler finally said she wanted him... the same, but also much different. More intense, less pubescent. Agnes had taken Noth out for dinner and then home herself for a little R and R. Trace hoped that she didn't go for MUCH older men.

The phone rang, the caller ID coming up with Harry Barniker. *Great.* Trace thought, *Just what I need now. An asshole chaser to weirdness and infatuation.*

"Hello?"

"Anderson." Barniker's voice rang out in all its fatuous dickheadedness. "I've decided to agree with the archeologists. This kind of find could be great PR for the building, despite the hold up in construction. I think it is worth having a look at. Meet me tomorrow with that expert archeologist who is on the case. What's her name?"

"Agnes," Trace coughed his surprise through his beer. "Argwhistle."

"Ah yes, please have her come along and we'll discuss the situation."

The phone went dead and Trace stared at it, hoping that an explanation would appear on its 'smart screen'. *What the hell? What's with the 180?* Something did not feel right for sure.

There was something in what Barniker said that simply did not jive. Trace went through the conversation again in his head, rattling it around. Suddenly he had it. Once you saw it, it stuck out like a sore thumb. Trace had known that asshole for a goodly time now and NEVER in all that time had he used the word 'please'. No way. That word was like a cross to the undead to Barniker. He'd rather have his eyelids ripped off than to ever use 'please' and 'thank you'. He just barked orders and expected through the sheer force of his will to get things done. What the hell was going on? It felt less than right.

Something was wrong. Trace had trusted his instincts since he was a kid and refused once to go on a roller coaster. He just had had a bad feeling about it. A week later the thing had flown off the track and killed a half dozen people. He felt the same thing now, that sense of wrongness. The pit of his stomach was beginning to roil. He grabbed the phone and punched Agnes's number.

"Hello?", she answered.

"Where are you?"

"Almost home, Mr. Anderson."

"Where's Noth?"

"I left him some time ago. Why?"

Trace filled her in on Barniker. She seemed thrilled about the back down, until he explained the 'please'.

"Don't go home. Not yet." He urged. "I know it sounds crazy but I have a bad feeling. Can you meet me?"

Agnes hesitated for a moment. "I don't know, this all sounds so weird. Perhaps you have been reading too many trashy novels, Mr. Anderson. People don't behave like that in real life."

"Okay, and in the real world you don't go to dinner with 15000 year old aliens."

There was a pause and he could almost hear Agnes rolling his logic around in her exquisite brain. "Point taken, Mr. Anderson"

Agnes told him her location and they settled on a place not too far from there; a roadside restaurant Trace knew of in that area.

After hanging up, Trace threw on his shoes and coat, grabbed his keys and headed for the door. As an afterthought, he went back to his bed and reached underneath for an old rusty tin box he kept there. Inside was an old pistol passed down from his father, a Walther p-38K that he had wrestled off an SS Captain in the war. He grabbed the extra ammo and stuffed it all in his jacket. Trace wasn't a fan of the gun, he didn't consider himself a cowboy or any such thing. He'd never used it on anyone for show or otherwise. He had killed a few cans with the amigos last summer when they took a sojourn in the desert. Mostly the damage on that trip was to his liver.

Trace made his way across the trailer then stopped at the sound of a knock at the door. A most unmanly involuntary squeak escaped Trace's throat. He froze for a moment.

"Trace? You in there? It's Vince."

Trace's bowels returned to their nesting place from his throat. Vince Meister was his on-site mechanic. Kept the monsters machines running smoothly. He had continued working through the shutdown to catch up and he usually worked late. He threw open the door. Vince stood there in all his monster size. Everything about him was gigantic. Trace was not a little guy but he felt like a child next to this brother. Tree trunk legs held up a massive Buick sized torso. Meat locker arms exploded out of boulder-sized shoulders ending in hands the size of dinner plates. His elephantine head nestled impressively atop the heap. Trace looked up at him at eye level even though he was standing at the bottom steps to the trailer, and thought of bugs on a windshield.

"Vince, buddy, what can I do for you?"

"Having trouble with the D-9, I was wondering if you could help me out."

Vince's voice was the only thing that belied his size. It was a soft tenor that tended to drift to falsetto land when he laughed. Trace had heard him sing once when he was alone in the shop. Brought tears to the eyes, that voice. Didn't say anything though because he'd seen him angry once also. Picked up a Volkswagen Beetle that had blocked his truck in. Picked it up and rolled it over. Impressive and scary.

Trace walked down the steps after securing the trailer.

"Since when do you need my advice on a fix Vince?"

He took a few steps around the trailer then, and stopped when he saw the others. Five of his guys were standing by the closed catering truck. Deevo Stengen, Simon Terazo, the Pizelli twins Diego and Chuck, and Carlo Swanson. They were a posse who hung around together. They called themselves 5 guys named Moe- kind of like the 'three amigos' and Trace. Except these guys were a lot rougher. They didn't consider it a successful weekend if there wasn't a broken bone and a whore at the end of it. The 5 of them actually called each other Mo. *A little weird for sure.* Weirder still, was that they should be standing outside his trailer at this hour, especially since the shutdown.

"Gentlemen." Trace met their eyes and stop cold. *Fuck.* There was something there, or rather not there. They were all a little glazed. Not pissed glazed though, weird glazed, like those creepy ventriloquist puppets. *Fuck again.*

Trace always trusted his instincts. And right now his insides screamed at him to act. *NOW.*

Trace charged forward taking Deevo by surprise as he lunged into his guts and kept moving. The twins recovered first from their surprise and punched toward his head. Trace ducked and they slammed knuckles into each other. Pushing through, Trace squared off with Carlo who produced a hammer from his jacket and swung it at his face. Trace dodged to the right and heard the hammer swoosh then felt the surprise of pain as it connected with the tip of Trace's shoulder.

Pain exploded through him as he continued toward the ground into a roll that brought him back on his feet. Trace caught Carlo on the side of the face with his fist. He went down and Trace scrambled as the others recovered and made their way over to him. Fortunately, Vince, for all his size was really slow, but as he looked in his direction he barely had time to duck as a heavy tool box, thrown by him, sailed through the air over his head, hitting fortunately, Deevo square in the temple. Deevo went down like a rice paper lantern under an elephant, twins stumbled over him as he fell.

Trace took the one second advantage to make his escape. He ran towards the parking lot where his truck was parked. He reefed open the door and threw himself inside, locked it, then scrambled for his keys, fumbling as they dropped on the floor. Then something slammed onto the hood of his truck. He looked up to see that the giant, Vince, had thrown himself over the hood and was standing up holding a metal rod in his hand. Trace looked into the rear-view mirrors and saw the twins on either side of the truck, making their way to his window with hammers in their hands. Trace finally got the key into the ignition. The engine roared to life and he dropped it into drive and punched the pedal.

The truck lurched forward throwing Vince violently from his standing position on his hood and he landed on the ground, the pipe impaling him through the stomach in the process. Trace cried out at the sheer violence of what just happened to him, but continued forward spraying the twins with gravel, as he made his getaway.

Jack's eatery had all the charm of fly shit. Agnes sat on the torn vinyl seat staring into the past. A long Formica counter sided with rusted chrome and ringed about with fixed stools commanded the room. Booths hugged the windows, each table set with sugar and salt and menu for customers that no longer came. The place didn't have the decency to know it was dead. Neither did the owner. A bag of bones wrapped in sagging white skin tottered precariously behind the counter puttering with the coffee machine. The only customer was a blue-rinsed old lady sitting at the bar reading a newspaper with a cartooned sized magnifying glass. Every now and then she would mutter something from the paper's contents. "Here's a one bedroom, 58 thou."

The old man muttered back "Beach side?"

"No friggin' way beach-side. For 58? You daft old shit, Dave. Nobody gonna sell beach side for 58. Shit." She looked around with rheumy eyes at Jack's Eatery, barely glancing at Agnes. Apprasising eyes, hopeful of a final escape before the ultimate escape. "We'd be friggin' lucky to get jack-shit for this dump."

The old guy, Dave muttered something unintelligible then clanked an ancient cup down on the counter and filled it with coffee. He made his way over to Agnes's booth, the cup chattering threateningly on its saucer. Agnes realized she was holding her breath when he finally reached the table and set it down.

"Can I get you anything else Miss?" The old blue eyes looked hopeful that Agnes could make a small contribution to dent that 58000.

"I, uh...I'll have a banquet burger...thanks"

The old eyes lit up and a surprisingly youthful smile beamed down on her. Agnes was sure he'd catch a quick peek at her boobs, but they remained fixed on her face. A gentleman.   "And a piece of apple pie, if you have it."

"Yes Mam! Comin' right up. Name's Dave by the way. Welcome to Jack's." The old guy sauntered away with a bit more pep in his step. She tried the coffee and to her surprise was delicious. Agnes smiled. She hoped that Trace would be hungry, as she had no intention of eating.

Trace Anderson. There was an interesting specimen. Agnes had found her thoughts returning again and again to him. Not her type, to be sure, but then, did she really have a type? Mostly she dated corporate guys, never colleagues. Well once, but that had ended in disaster when she found pictures of his Peruvian wife in his bedside drawer. Another Jerk. The corporate guys were jerks too, rich and full of the sound of their important voices. They spent money on her like it was air. Like that was going to impress her. Somehow the fancy blazer dudes were so taken with their own spending power, so wrapped up in their own delusions of adequacy.

But Trace was oddly different. Nice looking, rough around the edges, but not rude. There was a sensitive boy lurking in there that kept watch on his own vulnerability. *When that one hatched to manhood, there might be something there...but no. Come on Agnes, you have better things to do with your time. Important things.* Regardless of that square jaw and ruggedly gentle hands and that curly hair...Agnes snapped out of her thoughts as the door to the diner slammed open and Trace stumbled in. His shirt around his shoulder was bloody and he looked like hell. And scared, an emotion she hadn't considered on that face.

"Agnes! We've got to go...NOW!"

"What's going on...what do you mean?"

Agnes searched his face for answers. "What is going on, Anderson?"

"I'll explain later. Come on." Agnes had just enough time to reach inside her wallet and throw down a hundred dollar bill for Dave's trouble. Anderson grabbed her hand and pulled her out of the booth, half dragging her to the exit.

The old lady behind at the counter piped up. "Now look here boy-o, that is no way to treat a lady! You get your hands offa her!."

Agnes turned in Trace's grip to assure the old lady. Before the words were out her mouth. However, the opposite entrance to the diner opened and a giant entered flanked by two very mad looking men in construction clothes. Dave came out of the kitchen then with a platter load of food.

"Hello gentlemen, sit anywhere"

The old lady rounded on Dave.

"Dave you dipshit, these men aren't here to eat...they..."

Before the old lady could finish her sentence the big guy slammed the platter out of Dave's hands and shoved him hard in the direction of the bar. Dave went down behind the counter with a groan. The old lady let out a cry of Davey! Before turning on the big guy.

"You big shit, what do you have to go picking on an old man like that?"

The big guy raised his fist to punch the old lady when Trace let out a yell, letting go of Agnes's arm and hurling himself across the restaurant. The big guy turned away from the old lady as Trace plowed himself into him, tackling him backward.

Then all hell broke loose.

Agnes started toward Trace but a sound from behind stopped her. The other door had opened and two more construction dudes had entered behind her. One of them grabbed her from behind wrapping his meaty forearm around her neck trying to choke her. She acted quickly, thanking her parents in the movement for the fifteen years of karate they dragged her to. She brought her heel forward, then drove it back hard into her assailants lower leg, hearing a bone crack, the arm go slack and her attacker go down groaning.

The other guy who had been right behind the first tripped forward over his buddy and Agnes took the opportunity to drive her knee into his face as hard as she could. He went down in a heap then, she froze as a shot rang out. Agnes turned just in time to see the big guy go down, a small circle of red between his eyes. Trace turned toward one of the first two guys who tried to jump for cover. Another shot missed him as he dove over the counter the bullet ricocheting off the chrome and into the kitchen. The second guy tried to grab Trace from behind knocking the gun out of his hands, but Agnes, who had made her way over to that side of the restaurant, leveled a foot into his ribcage causing him to grunt and release Trace who finished him with a punch to the nose. The guy who had jumped over the counter now rose up and, while Trace and Agnes were engaged tried to edge his way over to where they stood.

"Don't fucking move moron!" The pumping of a shotgun stopped the last guy and brought Trace and Agnes's attention around. From behind the counter Dave stood, blood trickling down his cheek. Everyone froze. The old lady went over and picked up Trace's gun from the floor and leveled it at Trace and Agnes.

Dave spoke. "I don't know who the hell you people are, but you've made a hell of a mess. Everyone OUT! Now!"

The group of construction workers along with Trace and Agnes groaned and shuffled their way to the nearest exit prodded along by Dave and his pistol-packing woman.

The group was lined up in the parking lot, their backs to the restaurant, Dave and his woman standing guard over them.

From is pocket, Dave produced a cell phone put it on speaker phone and carefully dialed 911 as he kept the gun trained on his captives. The operator answered, Dave looked away for a moment, as he did so one of the construction men lunged forward and reached for Dave's shotgun.

It was the last thing he ever did.

The old woman cried out "Look out Dave!" and leveled Traces Gun at him, Dave also looked up as his assailant grabbed the barrel of the gun and tried to wrench it out of Dave's hand. Dave's finger squeezed and the gun went off shearing off the side of the workers face. The old lady, at the same time, let out a yell and fired her weapon, but missed her intended target. The bullet sailed between Trace and Agnes, narrowly missing them, went through the window, into the kitchen and punctured the gas main connected to the grill.

The explosion that rocked the restaurant was terrific. Those facing the window were thrown into the parking lot, shattered glass slitting skin, taking Dave and the old lady with them. A fire ball reached up into the night sky as the entire party were scattered, some moving, some not.

Some time later, Trace came to and found himself in a strange sitting position not far from his truck. He was bleeding in a dozen places, disoriented, and relatively deaf in both ears from the sound of the explosion. He shook his head and searched for Agnes. He found her on the other side of the truck, unconscious but still alive.

Without waiting or looking around he picked her up and threw her in the passenger side of the truck, then scampered over to the drivers side and climbed in.

Through the windshield, as he started the engine, he surveyed the damage.

Deevo and Carlo were charred corpses somehow having taken the brunt of the fireball; Simon was crawling away from the wreckage bleeding profusely. One of the twins was shaking the other's body, desperate for a response. Trace couldn't see the old couple anywhere and hoped like hell they were all right. He put the truck in gear and floored it out of the parking lot. As he passed the entrance he finally saw the older couple helping each other to their feet, then move towards an ancient Chevy Vega, clearly making their getaway, lest their attackers wished to finish them off. Trace hoped they had insurance on the place as he sped out of the parking lot and into the night.

SEVEN: The Colonel

What in the name of all that is good was going on? So
this was he and Agnes's first date. Yep, passed out and
covered in lacerations, after not eating in a restaurant. *Yeah
I'm a real Casanova.*

Trace looked and noticed the fuel gauge getting ugly
to empty and switched over to the reserve tank. No way in
hell he was stopping now, not until he'd put some major
miles from the goons and done some serious straightening
out of all this crap. He also wanted to get hold of Noth and
get a few straight answers.

The miles cruised by and his thoughts lead him in
great swirling loops of panic and terror. He realized he
could be pretty tough when he was facing down a dead rat
or yelling at the guys to get back to work, but people trying
to kill him, explosions and real pain, kind of made him a
little squeamish. Agnes stirred in the seat beside him. He
reached over and touched the top of her head. She came to
sputtering and thrashing making him swerve a little on the
road.

"Take it easy, lady"

"What just happened? Where the hell are we? What is
going on?" She punched him in the arm. His bad arm.

"Ow...fuck. What is your deal?"

"I'm just frustrated for shit...dammit." She punched
him again.

"Okay, okay. Calm down and let me let you in on
some of it...jeez."

Agnes looked all long-eyed at him, still beautiful but
icy. He filled her in on the history of my evening with 'the
boys' up to the point his butt ended up on the ground.

She seemed to need to process the whole event. Trace,
on the other hand was a little ticked off by the whole affair.

"Where's Noth? He must have some answers here. I've known those guys for a while now. They're assholes, but not thugs. They had this glazed over look like zombies. Knew me and didn't at the same time." He shuddered involuntarily at the thought of the mindless pit workers trying to end him.

"I'll call him now." Agnes pulled her phone out of a neat little pocket that was cleverly hidden inside her skirt and dialed. Noth was not there.

"I'll leave him a message, where should I tell him we are going...where are we going...how long have we been driving?"

"Just tell him to call us. I don't want that info out there. Trace switched on the radio and dialed to the news station.

Some overly resonant upbeat voice was doing an update on the UV index. Next, the news came. The explosion at the restaurant had been reported and the authorities were investigating. They seemed to have very little information and were appealing to the public to come forward with information.

"Dammit. Shit."

"We should go to the cops, Mr. Anderson"

"And tell them what, about aliens and body possession? What about my guys who tried to kill us? No, we don't know if anyone involved in the police are being controlled by Krynos. We need Noth and answers. Meantime, I have an old friend not far from here, in an out of the way place, who should be able to help."

Agnes considered his brilliant out loud thinking and finally nodded slowly in agreement. Even dusty and unkempt, her hair trestles tickled the side of her jaw in a most alluring way. *Man...to be a freckle on that jaw.*

"Alright Mr. Anderson. We will do it your way. I hope it is the right way."

Trace nodded. A mile up the road, he turned off on a side road and spent the next 20 minutes winding through back roads and non-roads to arrive at our destination.

"Here we are. Home of the kindest most brilliant jackass you'll ever meet."

Agnes rolled her eyes. "Great. You mean more than you?"

Trace smiled at her. *Progress made. A good day in the end.*

Colonel Cranston J. Eldbarge enjoyed his arboretum. He actually loved the word, seeing a sign for it on a highway once, he pulled over wondering what it was. When he discovered it was a place to collect trees he was hooked. Cranston loved trees. They were the perfect soldiers. They didn't talk back and they never fell out of the perfect formation he planted them in. If the weather bombarded them they never ran away or got disoriented. They could face down the toughest lightning mortar and not move. If a comrade did fall to the often-superior forces of nature, the others never wavered.

They soldiered on. On each tree he had placed the names of every soldier that had died under his command. He served in three wars and saw more action than most. He saw men die in every way possible, their eyes glazing to oblivion after the shock of wounding. Somehow, the fates had been on his side. Shouldn't have been considering the situations he had found himself in. When Trace Atkinson's truck came down his road, he had no idea he would be drawn back into service.

Lithe rather than bulky, Cranston was a band of iron. His spine was ram-rod straight and there wasn't an ounce of fat on him. His angle iron jaw supported a lean face that was still handsome and rugged. A fair amount of grey had crept into his hair, but hadn't disappeared. He kept it in a strict two by four regulation cut that he did himself; no small feat.

The truck rolled down the gravel path between his sentries of Wollemi pines, a rare and beautiful gift from an old friend down under. Also beautiful was the redhead that came out of the truck with Trace. Cranston felt his spine straighten even more at the sight of her. As they got closer, however, he saw their distress.

After shaking hands with Trace he turned for introductions to the woman.

"You, young lady, are a vast improvement on the imported beer and a jar of clear death fluid he normally brings." He smiled his half hitch smile, the one that showed a dimple in his left cheek and was rewarded with a smile back. Worked every time. "Call me Cranston."

Trace cut in. "I never notice you complain about the booze, Colonel, thought you'd like a better host gift."

Trace's attempt at humour, Cranston noticed, garnered him a delicious scowl from Agnes. Cranston knew in a moment that she liked him.

"Pleasantries aside, I can tell this isn't your average visit. You both look like shit, no offense Agnes."

"None taken...Cranston. I've had quite a day with your friend here."

The Colonel snorted at the comment.

"Trace is a good boy, Agnes, hasn't quite figured out females yet. Give him time, he'll come around. Let's go inside and get you cleaned up, then we can talk."

Agnes speared him with a dazzling smile and a grateful thank you as they moved into the house.

An hour later, Cranston had seen to their minor wounds and needs and now sat stunned at the story Trace had just laid out for him.

He looked from one to the other waiting for a punch line that never came. The implications of the story raised hairs on his head.

"Your not bull-shitting me are you?"

"No sir."

"Dammit Trace I've known you since you were a baby...how is your Dad by the way?"

"He's fine. Not happy about the home."

"Good man. I served under him in Korea. I was a young piece of bullshit. He beat that out of me in about a minute and a half. Saved my life once. Did I ever tell you that story, Trace?"

"Once..."

"Or twice or a thousand, probably. Okay, I'm old but not stupid. Let's get on with this little mission of yours."

Action plans began springing up in his head. First though, he needed some intel. He motioned them over to his computer and pulled up the diner story and everything he could on troop movement's a.k.a. what the state troopers were doing.

"Where can we find this Noth man...alien?" He looked over at Agnes.

"You surprised I didn't raise an eyebrow at the alien? Remind me to tell you about my time in area 51. I've seen shit that would make your beautiful hair uncurl."

Agnes actually giggled. The last time she giggled was when she met Brad Pitt at a fancy gala her friend had tickets for. Something about this Colonel, old yes, but still hadn't lost it. Here was the kind of man that came from an era of real men and women. She liked that. Didn't demean a woman, but was able to make a woman feel like a woman. Her father had had that same way about him with her mother, a strong, successful woman in her own right, but enjoying and embracing her womanhood, not feeling a need to be like a man. She looked at Trace, rugged also, still a boy, but he was showing the promise of future manhood...

"Agnes?" Trace snapped her out of her musings."

"Hmmm....what?"

"I said, can you get hold of him?"

"Who?"

"You all right? That bump on the head scramble your brains? I said, could you contact Noth?"

"Noth, of course." She reached into her purse and pulled out her cell. There was no service.

The Colonel noticed her cell troubles. "Sorry, hate the damn things. One of those phone companies wanted to put up a cell tower on my land. They got the business end of an ak-47."

Agnes put the phone down on the table, and then remembered something. "Wait a minute. Noth gave me this." She reached into her purse and pulled what looked like a black multifaceted die.

"What is it?" The Colonel asked.

"Noth said it was his calling card."

Trace took it between his fingers and felt the solidity of it. It was polished like a diamond, with neat markings on its surface.

He handed it over to Cranston. "Ever seen anything like that?"

"Nope, don't recognize the writing either. Looks like the kind of dice those geeks use in strategy games; let's see"

Cranston tossed the die onto the mahogany table they were sitting at. The die skipped across the surface stopping with one of the strange squiggles on the top. Cranston was just about to pick it up, when the markings began to pulse red. It glowed red for about thirty seconds then the letters changed to a brilliant white. After another thirty seconds the markings faded and the die returned to its original state.

Two hours later, Colonel Cranston was shaking hands with what he believed to be his first alien.

<\>

After all these years, Noth still could not get used to humans. He didn't dislike them, they just...felt different. Alien. After all these years, Noth still felt homesick. He had left a lot behind, Friends, family, lovers...much of which was gone. *Funny how you could miss what no longer existed. Or did it?* His religion taught of alternate realities. That death didn't exist, one simply...shifted to a new place, a new reality, what we considered our current world was, in fact many worlds, many mind places...but solid, real. After so many years among humans, Noth still found solace in his religion. His time was not infinite. He would eventually die, fifteen or twenty thousand years from now he would fade and move on.

He looked around at his new companions. Agnes with her fiery hair and solid disposition, very beautiful. He had taken lovers in his years here on Earth; careful not to stay too long. Agnes was looking for love, a love Noth would never be able to pursue in his own life. She was drawn to this Trace fellow, they were drawn to each other, but neither could yet figure out the path. Trace was a boy-man-child. He moved easily between the stages of man, but couldn't seem to settle on one, each stage fleeing from another.

Finally, there was the newest addition. The Colonel. Noth had known a lot of military people in his career. Had even been in the military from time to time, as necessity in his mission dictated. They were an interesting breed. Similar in approaches to situations, but different in their motivations. Anger or caring. That was the difference.

Those military people he met over the years, those who came from a place of anger wanted to bull their way through life, couldn't conceive of other perspectives. They had their own agenda and wanted to bend the world to their will.

However, those in the military that came from a place of caring, were the ones that Noth could work with. They had an intuitive understanding of people; could shift perspectives as need dictated by those around them. People followed these types willingly: would die for them. Noth knew in a few moments that the Colonel was one of those. He looked around at the other three and was still amazed at how people found each other. Humans said it was chance, but Noth knew better. Like-minded people found each other; their energies pulled them together for good or for ill.

The Colonel fed them all, an incredible stew supplemented with generous glasses of red wine. They sat relaxing for the first time in what felt like a long time around the Colonel's spacious kitchen. A Korean man he had met during the war had designed the Colonel's house. He liked to call the style, Western Asian: a log cabin Hanok. He settled them around his big round teak table and gave them spiked hot chocolate and let his three guests get him up to speed. Afterwards the Colonel simply nodded and asked 'what now?'

Noth smiled. *Like finding like.*

The Colonel asked a series of detailed questions, looking for a clear picture, including his concern over the explosion at the diner.

"No need to concern yourself over that. I have dealt with that situation. The owners have been presented with a very generous offer for their silence and to aid in covering up the attack."

Agnes couldn't help but smile over the thought of the two old people finally getting the retirement they so longed for.

"What about the guys that were chasing us? What happened to them?" Trace asked.

"Unfortunately, Krynos had no further use for them, so he had them meet with some unfortunate accidents." The three humans got quiet then, the reality of what they were engaged in sinking in.

The Colonel blew through his lips. He had lost men before, seen them die on both sides. It was never easy, the only way forward was to focus on the task at hand. "So these keys, the one's Krynos needs to fully release himself...where are they, Mr. Noth?"

"They are scattered throughout the world, I have taken many years to hide them. The trouble is we have much less time to recover them. They leave a trail back to the prison, but I have obscured it as much as I am able. As I said, Krynos will pour his energy and his resources into finding them. As luck would have it, his number one, this Eddy person, is the first in the chain of his minions. His mind is inferior to many and Krynos will have to be lead him around by the nose."

"Why doesn't he just kill him and start with someone smarter?" Trace asked.

Noth nodded. "A good question. Fortunately he cannot destroy the first link in the chain only build from there."

"And those that die along the way?" Said Agnes.

"They can be replaced. He will weaken with every new recruit, but still has the power to influence enough to make life very difficult for us. Those he brought against you two so far will be replaced with stronger and more formidable foes."

"Like state troopers or trained soldiers?" Said the Colonel.

"Precisely. The only way is to find the Keystones before Krynos does."

"And destroy them." I said.

Noth raised a hand. "No, they must be brought back to the statue and he must be resealed. One cannot destroy chaos, only contain it."

It was Agnes's turn for questions. She had been sipping a giant mug of spiked cocoa supplied by the Colonel.

"Can't you go and get them? You know where they are, after all."

Noth shook his head.

"Krynos can trace me. For now, we are safe. I have obscured our trails as much as possible. My power is also linked to the cave, the farther away I get from it the weaker I become. He is searching for the keys and will find it eventually; our only hope is to get to them first. My only hope is that someone can retrieve the keys for me. For us."

"So what do we do?" Trace asked. "Split up and get as many as possible?"

"No, Mr. Anderson. They must be found in order."

Frustrated, Trace stood up and paced the Colonel's kitchen.

"That's a lot of rules for a superior alien race. No, I'm just saying, we put a dude on the moon in ten years, you'd think in 5000 years they would have come up with a better system to contain the most destructive force in the universe."

Noth nodded his understanding.

"I am sure there have been advances as you say. Unfortunately you forget I am a alone. I don't receive...updates."

"Where is the first Keystone?" The Colonel asked.

"In a remote jungle location."

"How the heck do we get there?

The Colonel offered his support to the situation. "Perhaps, young man, that is where I come in..."

All eyes swung to the Colonel. "Let me make some calls. I have some very interesting friends. I can get us out of the USA and to wherever, but we will need resources at the locations as well."

"I have considerable resources in the world also, Colonel. I'm sure between us, we should be able to properly outfit this mission."

There was a pause among the group as everyone considered the enormity of what they were setting out to try to accomplish.

It was the Colonel who broke the silence.

"I think however, you are leaving out a very important piece of information Mr. Noth and I am curious as to why you are hiding it."

Trace and Agnes exchanged a worried look with each other.

"Hiding what?" Trace said.

The Colonel had not taken his eyes off his eyes off Mr. Noth. "Haven't you two youngsters forgotten to ask a very important question of Mr. Noth? Why you two? You aren't particularly trained for this kind of thing. Of all the suitable people in the world with training and know how, why did you pick them, Mr. Noth?"

Noth looked back at the Colonel, surprised by his insight.

He took a deep breath and decided they all deserved a truthful, straightforward answer.   "It's very simple. I need them for their expertise, their resourcefulness and one important thing, I may have forgotten to mention. You see, Agnes and Trace contain my DNA."

It was Trace who recovered first from the shock of this recent revelation.

"Whoa, wait a minute here. What are you saying? You mean we have some Mylogen blood in us, the same way Eddy Smiter has Keldar DNA? How is that possible? I thought you said you didn't get 'involved' with the locals, Mr. Noth? Are you telling me you are my fifty times great great Grandpappy?"

For the first time, Noth was at a loss for words. When he spoke his voice was tinged with shame.

"You are correct, Mr. Anderson. We share a genetic past. I'm afraid that it is not as easy as I make it appear to be alone and trapped on a planet, many millions of miles away from my home for thousands of years. I did find…companionship over the millennia. Unfortunately I was not as careful as I had thought I was. Accidents do happen."

Trace smiled kindly. "Mr. Noth. Well, well. How very human of you."

Noth cleared his throat, "I'll take that as a compliment, Mr. Anderson."

Agnes leaned forward then. "But how did you know about our DNA? And for that matter what does it matter?"

A line of tension appeared around Trace's jaw. "Good point, you're not planning to invade our bodies are you?"

Mr. Noth held up a hand. "No, heavens no, that is not my intention at all. As to your first question, as I have told you I am a very resourceful person. I have spent much time in locating the genetic line of my unfortunate indiscretions. When the prison cracked, I was 'notified', shall we say. It was a strike of pure chance that both of you should contain the necessary genetic make-up required."

"Required for what Mr. Noth?" said the Colonel.

"Required to operate the Keystones."

Trace abruptly stood up and pushed his hand through his hair. "Wait a minute here. You want us to not only find them, but help you use them?"

"Yes Mr. Anderson. I need your help. We are already to far ahead in this, I'm afraid. I will entertain getting others, but I'm afraid that we won't have the time we need in order to succeed." It was Noth's turn to lean forward, for the first time a pleading look spread across his face. "I need you both. I can't operate the keystones alone, I need three.

"I don't suppose you could use me, Mr. Noth?" said the Colonel.

"Unfortunately no, you do not contain Mylogen DNA."

"Not sure whether I'm disappointed or happy at that news, Mr. Noth." Said the Colonel. He looked over at Agnes and Trace seeing apprehension in their faces. "Well kids. I guess it's up to both of you. Are you in or out? By the way, no shame in saying no…from either of you."

Noth looked around at this small gathering of humans. He liked what he saw in each of them, but was dismayed at what he was asking them to do and at his deception. "I agree with the Colonel here. As you've guessed, this is extremely dangerous. I do not know what, as your kind says, in the cards for us, but the future of mankind is in our hands."

Three humans nodded their understanding of what he was telling them.

Trace smiled at Agnes. "Well, Agnes, want to go on an adventure with me?" He gave her a half-hitched cheesy smile that made Agnes roll her eyes.

"For the sake of Archeology everywhere, I will agree to put up with him and go along." Agnes said.

Trace gave an exaggerated wince then smiled. "Ouch. Well for the sake of Construction workers everywhere, I'll let Agnes Tag along. Let's do this!"

The Colonel nodded his head also. "Super. Let's get to work then. We have a lot of planning to do."

EIGHT: The Tree

Noth left the Colonel a few hours after Trace and Agnes got on their way. He had taken Agnes aside and given her three Keystones and some instruction into what they were to be used for. He didn't want to give too much detail, in case one of them was captured. He knew that they would figure it out as they went along, Trace had already proven himself a capable improviser and Agnes was cool under pressure. The Colonel and he had spent some time after the pair got on their way, pooling their considerable resources to support Trace and Agnes on their quest.

He liked the Colonel, which surprised him. Most of the militarily minded he had met over his long life had left him repulsed. They seemed so sure of themselves all the time. Their surety was based on the belief that might would make right; that any situation could be muscled to a forgone conclusion. It was shocking how many times they had been proved wrong in this belief, yet even after the final reckoning, after the dead were counted and the mission or war was considered a failure or a draw, they continued on believing that if they only had more muscle they could have 'won'. The Colonel was different, however. He was more akin to the martial artist. One who despised violence, and would only use it as a last resort, to protect not to conquer.

"It's real easy to come up with an excuse to use force." He had said. "Many of the leaders, military and political I came across, acted like some kind of moral authority. Made me sick. Bringing in God and religion and all that, like it was a heartfelt need to 'make right', by killing a bunch of young men and women. Then there were the Cowboys that wanted to use the latest gun or fire off their new missile, or just go in making a shitload of noise with

their guns. Yeah, I talked a lot of guys into other ways to
'get the job done'. And those under you appreciated it.
Knew they were more likely to stay alive with me than
some. They wanted to make me a general, pull me out of
the field and all. I told them to go fuck themselves, no way
I was leaving them. Felt I couldn't protect them if I wasn't
there, if I was making decisions from a distance. Guess I'm
an old mother hen at that."

Noth had given the Colonel instructions regarding the
black cube. Through it, Noth would communicate
instructions and keystone locations to him. From there the
Colonel would coordinate the details.

"I have access to a system of magnifiers. Sort of like
your primitive cell phone network. From there I can
channel my energies where I need. But my resources are
limited, Colonel. I only wish I could gather the Keystones
myself. Krynos's escape was...not expected. Our hope lies
in Trace and Agnes, we must watch over them at all costs."

"I'll take good care of those kids, Mr. Noth. Anderson
is like a son to me."

The two shook hands and parted ways.

The attack from Krynos came about ten miles away
from Noth's remote home. Noth almost swerved off the
road as a wave of energy hit the shield he'd been
maintaining. Powerful, like a boulder being thrown at an
acrylic dome. Normally his shielding would have easily
held, but because he was also dispensing his energy to
protect Trace and Agnes, the keys location, and the
Colonel, he was stretched pretty thin. Noth managed to get
the car to the side of the road as he collapsed in his seat and
went deep inside his consciousness to do battle. As he
slowed his breathing he moved to transform as he had done
so many times. He didn't even think about it, had been

trained thousands of years ago. He shed his corporeal body like removing clothing. Slipped out of his body, keeping only a thin thread to connect him back. In his energy form he entered Chas, the world of energy that holds the physical world together.

Slam! Another energy assault rammed into his dome. *So strong.* Noth raced to fortify, knowing that he couldn't sustain it forever. He had no body to speak of; he could be infinitely big or small as he wished; yet doing so would expend energy. He prepared for another assault, when it came he was ready his awareness was everywhere at once.

An instant before he was hit, he sensed it and pinpointed the location, then concentrated everything him he had on that area. Noth reversed his shield and concentrated all his energy for a brief moment lasting no longer than the speed of thought. Kind of like instantly erecting an elastic cup that rebounded the energy full force back to the attacker. Doing so was extremely dangerous, if he was off by the slightest fraction his shield would fail and all would be lost. The energy hit precisely the point he had predicted. The weight of rebounding an energy attack like this was extremely draining and just as the last of the assault left the cup a tiny amount spilled over.

A tendril grabbed on to a small piece of Noth's energy and yanked like a fish on a hook. Noth struggled against the line, flailing, feeling himself being pulled away towards oblivion. At the same time he began to sense a presence probing into his essence; a cold and ruthless hand reaching into his protective barriers searching for a weakness. Another tug and Krynos extended himself more and began to sift and suck at Noth's mind, searching for clues and images that Noth fought to keep inviolable.

Noth could feel his defenses weakening and Krynos's energy probing deeper. He decided to gamble again, knowing that what he planned would leave him utterly vulnerable. Like a fish on a hook, Noth let himself relax completely, ceasing for a moment his struggle. Surprised, Krynos hesitated, and in that moment Noth struck. In one last desperate surge he went on the attack. Pouring most of his energy into a repellant blast. Krynos, unprepared for that instant was thrown back into a retreat that expended his energy and forced him to flee. As he retreated however he snatched at one image in Noth's mind.

The image of a tree.

NINE: Jungle Fever

Riding in a cargo plane wasn't really as much fun as Trace thought it would be. There was no in-flight movie and the food was leftover corn hash the Colonel had assembled for their dinner. Agnes and he had parted their ways at around two o'clock in the morning and hopped through about a dozen small airstrips in a variety of winged transportation. Some of them were barely held together, Trace was surprised his stomach did.

The Colonel arranged some fake paper work for them, then went his own way, promising to connect when he could. No point for the entire team to be together, in case they needed a way out. Trace was happy to be with Agnes who, conversely, did not look happy to be with him. She seemed to be locked in a war of nausea over his presence. Noth disappeared shortly before their departure to places unknown. He had figured the less the rest knew about his whereabouts, the better, which somehow, made Trace more mentally queasy than the actual queasiness he felt as the plane dipped and banked along with the hashy contents of his stomach.

How the hell had his life turned to this, so fast? And why? He looked over at Agnes across from him, lovely even in the shade of skin green she was wearing, her hands clutching the fuselage, her jaw set in a determined grimace. *Beautiful. But was that it?* Trace refused to examine his feelings toward her, simply because he knew they would not come bouncing back in reciprocation.

But there was more to all this adventure than Agnes, beautiful and giddy-making though she was, she was a stranger and Trace felt the need to self-preserve. *No.* The real reason he didn't walk away that day in the cave was because of his father, a war veteran of two wars and a hero.

Trace's father had spent his entire life serving his country. Trace had been in awe of him since he was little. His voice was loud but generous, he filled a room with his presence, and others deferred to his opinion. He had always taught his son to trust his instincts. To fight the good fight, work hard and feel good about making a contribution to the world. Trace's father was the poster child for action.

After he retired he actually worked harder than he ever had, championing causes, especially those that seemed hopeless. Trace had worked along side of him, until his own work started taking him all over the world and time landed his father in a home. Trace missed those days working with his father. He wanted to get back to being an agent for change, but work made his days long and his excuses convenient.

That meeting in the cave seemed to unleash something in Trace. *I could do something that would be of value, I could make a difference.* An odd choice for him, he thought, when he could have worked for Unicef or a dozen other charities, but Trace wanted something of his own and different. *Well you couldn't get more different than this.* He looked over again at Agnes, and realized there were perks to charity work, he was about to offer his smoothest compliment to her when the plane banked again, lurching his libido into neutral. *That will have to wait.*

The plane began to descend. Noth had given them some background into the first location. Looked like a jungle to Trace. All he knew was that they had been moving south for about a day. The landing was the icing on the cake. Jarring his spine into a shape no chiropractor could fix. Agnes was ashen. Trace's knuckles were still white and he had to consciously pry them off the armrest.

The air outside was like a bathtub and the world was as green as he had ever seen. They were on a dirt road, not really a landing strip. As soon as they got off the plane with the packs that the Colonel had outfitted them with, the plane started up and began to taxi away. Neither Agnes nor Trace ever saw one pilot their whole trip.

There was an old surplus jeep waiting for them near the road. They climbed in after stowing their gear and Trace was happy to find a GPS unit. Alice called out navigation as they bumped along what could loosely be called a road.

"This friend of yours is pretty resourceful."

It was the first full sentence Alice had spoken to him since they first took off in the first plane.

"Hey she can do more than grunt."

Agnes smiled. "I didn't trust myself to open my mouth, lest the contents of my stomach should decorate you."

At that Trace laughed his head off.

"Yeah the colonel is a good man, he and my father go way back. They saw a lot of shit together." He stopped for a moment, letting everything wash over him. "Do you think we are doing the right thing? This all seems so crazy."

Agnes flashed those probing baby blues at him all serious-like. She looked at him as though she was examining some ancient carving and not liking the translation that popped into her mind. Finally she answered.

"I'm not sure myself. But what choice do we have? For some strange reason I trust Noth. When we had dinner together he told me a lot about his life. You can pack a lot of stuff in a few thousand years. Mostly though he just seemed sad. He left a life behind to come to our dingy little planet to be a guardian."

"A what?"

"A guardian. That's what they call his job."

"And these Keystones? Why couldn't he just destroy them?"

"Because they're indestructible. And even if they could be destroyed, they are somehow tied into our world.

Getting rid of them would somehow be disastrous for our planet."

"We're back to crazy." Trace said. Agnes didn't seem to like that particular phrase, so he decided to change the subject. What are we looking for anyway?"

"A tree."

Trace looked around at the thick jungle and was about to open my mouth.

"Before you get all smart-assy with me. A very particular tree. And a very old tree has been alive for a few thousand years."

"That's it? Is there a visitor information booth there?"

"Noth told me that there is more to this tree than meets the eye. Plus he gave me these. He told me they were keys of some kind."

Agnes held up three small, domino-shaped stones the size of her palm. They each glowed a different colour; pulsating red, blue, and yellow.

"He told me that the red one comes first, then the blue and finally the yellow."

Trace took the red one and held it up to the sun. The red light seemed to pulsate from deep within the stone.

"Wow. That is beautiful. What does it do?"

Agnes shrugged. "I'm not exactly sure. Noth said we would figure it out when we got to our destination." She looked down at the GPS unit. "Which is still quite a distance from here. Three miles north there is a fork in the road, turn left."

Twenty minutes later we hit a dead end. The path ended and beyond was a thick forest, green, lush and, to Trace's mind, very Indiana Jones.

"Okay, thank you for travelling with Trace Tours, hope you enjoy your stay, please see the concierge for your complimentary beverage before entering the pool."

Agnes gathered the GPS unit from the dash.

"Gather the gear, Anderson. Time to hoof it."

"Yes Ma'm!" He shouldered his pack and handed Agnes's to her. In the cargo trunk beneath the packs he uncovered a metal container. "What's in here?" Agnes looked over as Trace opened it up to reveal a small arsenal. "Care to start a war?"

After not a little argument Trace managed to convince her to take a small handgun.

Good Times...

Hiking into the jungle looked like fun on all those adventure movies, Trace thought. *A slight sheen of perspiration on the grim faced hero as he hacks disdainfully away at the undergrowth with a machete, while those that follow tiptoe mouse-like behind, slightly in love with their leader.*

The reality was much more crappy. Four hours in and Trace had twisted his ankle and given a pint of blood to dinosaur-sized bugs. He was sweating buckets, not perspiring, and panting like a puppy in the sun. *Not attractive.* Plus, Agnes was leading the way with her little GPS unit. *At least she had the decency to sweat. A little.*

Agnes held up the GPS unit for him to see. "We're getting close."

Trace narrowly missed getting whacked in the face by a branch Agnes had just pushed aside.

"What are we looking for?"

"That." Agnes stopped and was pointing ahead of her.

Up ahead, in a large clearing, was a solitary tree. The jungle seemed to stop 200 feet all around it, as though reverently bowing down to it.

Agnes started to walk into the clearing when Trace's hand grabbed her shoulder.

"Whoa there Tex. Let's take it slow here."

Agnes carefully disengaged herself. She wasn't a fan of being told what to do, but Trace's tone kept her from a witty retort.

"What's the problem?"

"Well let's see. I seem to recall a certain diner we did not have the pleasure of eating at. A real explosive affair if I recall..."

Agnes rolled her eyes.

"We are a million miles from nowhere, you don't honestly expect me to believe that we could have been followed? Hell, I barely know where we are."

The heat and the jungle were beginning to fray Trace's nerves, even with a beautiful girl. "Okay. Fine. Would you at LEAST meet me half way here." Trace reached into her pack and pulled out her gun. She rolled her eyes but took the gun, then sarcastically adopted her best search and rescue stance.

"What are you doing? You look like Quasimodo. Do you know how to fire that thing?"

"I'm a bloody Archeologist! Not an operative, damn it. Nor am I a trained killer."

"What you think I do this every damn day?" I shot back. "Gee, let's see, after constructing buildings I like to go out and shoot bad guys."

Agnes argued back waving the gun around as she gesticulated.

"Yeah, and when I'm done digging up ancient ruins, I work for the CIA."

Trace held up placating hands. Carefully stilling the Agnes's waving hands.

"Okay, okay! Here is the safety, here is the trigger." He said pointing at the gun. "This is where the bad, bad bullet comes out to stop the bad, bad men."

A storm rolled over Agnes's face, Trace plowed on.

"Look. I don't know what we may find. But I've already been ambushed twice, both times very unpleasant.

My feeling is that next time will be more unpleasant. Do whatever you like. Just don't shoot me in the process."

With that Trace pulled out his own gun and made his way into the clearing, circling, constantly watching the jungle. Agnes chose her own path, a straight line toward the tree, and got there before him.

"Wow, still in one piece." She retorted as he caught up with her.

"You know one day, you will thank me for saving your ass."

"Leave my ass out of this, Anderson. You don't fool me with your boy act. I've seen the way you gawk at me like I'm a medium rare steak."

"You've got to be kidding me, lady! I wouldn't be caught dead at that barbecue." Trace wasn't quite sure if that made sense, but it was the only thing he could think of as a retort. She wanted strictly business, then fine. He told her so, bringing his face within inches to hers; the two locking eyes.

Man, is she ever hot when she's mad.

His jaw is so fucking square, Agnes thought.

It was Trace that broke the silent tension.

"Are we done?"

"Yes."

"Good then let's see what the hell we came halfway around the world to look at a tree for."

After another moment of staring into each other's faces they broke contact and moved away to survey the tree.

The ancient tree was enormous, and incongruous in it's surroundings. Like it belonged on a different planet. Gnarled limbs stretched high into the sky ending in a deep canopy of oddly shaped leaves the size of a man's hand. Five people holding hands could barely make their way around the circumference of its trunk. The two walked around touching the knotted bark.

"What are we looking for?" Trace asked.

"I don't know." She held up the red rectangular stone that Noth had given her. "It has something to do with this."

For the first time, Trace noticed that the glowing red stone had something very small drawn on them, like writing.

"What do those markings mean?"

"Noth said they mean 'where the sky and the earth meet'."

"That's it? Didn't want to clue us into what that meant, I guess."

"He said we'd understand when the time came."

"Well, time is running short on us, in a little while we will be spending a dark night here. We only have about a half an hour before the sun goes down."

"Perhaps that's what it means. When the sky and the earth meet could mean sundown?"

"Darkness, the great equalizer...okay. Fine." Trace stood there, not trusting himself to speak. He was hot and cranky and was sure that Agnes felt the same. Standing there waiting for half an hour seemed like an eternity in his present state. "I'm going to... scout the area." Trace made to walk away.

"Good."

"Fine."

The two parted ways. Agnes sat on the ground to wait, pulling out a canteen and determinately avoided Trace's look. Trace walked around the perimeter of the clearing, searching for signs that someone had followed them in here. Perhaps she was right. Maybe he had over-reacted...only two people in the world knew where they were and the chances that someone had found the Colonel or Noth were pretty slim....

"Anderson!" Agnes's voice pierced through the dusk.

Trace ran over to the tree, gun in hand, and put his back to the trunk. Edging his way around he came face to face with Agnes.

"Jesus! Put that down."

"I heard you cry out. What happened?"

Agnes pointed toward the tree. "That."

Trace looked to where he pointed. In the glow of dusk the outline of a shape could be made out: a rectangular depression the same size as the medallion she was holding in her hand. The two looked at one another. Trace took hold of the red stone and held it up to the depression. The tree seemed to draw the stone towards it. It lodged itself into the tree and the bark around the circle began to glow, growing in size until it resembled a doorway. Then the light began to fade along with the bark, leaving a door into the tree itself.

Trace was very impressed by this piece of high tech.

"Well. That's cool. I've got to get one of those for my trailer. Save me from all those woman pounding down my door."

"You mean trying to get out?"

Agnes went into her pack and retrieved flashlights. "Come on Casanova. Let's go."

Trace and Agnes entered the tree to discover an ancient spiral staircase that wound down into the ground like a corkscrew. Several feet down the stairs opened into a giant stone cavern.

"Wow. This place is enormous!"

Trace looked above and noticed that the roots of the tree formed the ceiling to the cavern, extending out beyond what the eye could see.

As they neared the bottom the cavern broke off into many tunnels leading off into darkness.

Trace considered the options turning around trying to probe down the tunnels with his flashlight. "Okay pick a direction, I guess?"

Agnes held up the red stone. It was glowing. As she walked toward one of the tunnels the light seemed to fade.

She walked back and tried another. This time the medallion glowed brighter.

"I think this way."

"Show off. Okay lets follow the glowing rock."

Agnes had already set off before Trace could impress her with more of his witty remarks. He trudged after her, their footsteps echoing off the cavern walls.

A few minutes later the tunnel ended in another door. In the center of the door was another round depression the size of the medallion. Agnes placed the round disk into the hole and the door disappeared, the disk dropping to the ground. Trace retrieved it and set out ahead. The doorway led to a chamber. As Trace stepped across the threshold the entire chamber began to glow a soft sky blue. Both Trace and Agnes let out a gasp yet their voices made no echo. They were standing in an enormous radiant dome about 300 feet in diameter and perfectly spherical. It towered over their heads ending in a perfectly flat floor also glowing. His heart pounding, Trace went over and felt the walls.

"This is no material I know of. Look at this. It's perfectly smooth. It's incredible, the light seems to come from inside of it, rather than behind...and feel it-it's warm. I don't know who made this, but it certainly didn't come from Home Depot. It'd make a great countertop."

Agnes went over and touched the walls for herself. She had to admit; it was the most unusually impressive thing she had ever seen. She looked over at Trace for a moment who was caught up examining the surface. The look of wonder in his eyes made her smile. A fascinated boy with a new toy...in a man's body... Trace looked over and she snapped her eyes to the center of the dome. "Okay, when all this is over you and Noth can go into the countertop business." She quipped, hoping to cover her thoughts.

Trace's eyes lingered on Agnes for a moment, basking in the beauty of the dome's light on her face. *She made her thoughts clear earlier about how she felt about him, no point getting sucked in further.* Trace felt the sting of her sarcasm and also looked toward the center of the dome. In the center of the floor was yet another rectangular depression. Trace held out the red stone and looked at Agnes.

"Third time's a charm, I guess?"

Agnes shrugged in acquiescence. Trace knelt down and placed the red stone in the depression. This time there was a soft clicking sound as the hole swallowed it up. The dome's light changed to a darker blue and was pulsating. The circle of the hole began to grow, it's colour changing to crimson. Trace and Agnes stepped back as the circle grew in size to around six feet, and then began to grow upwards into the chamber. A cylinder of red colour, rose up toward the ceiling, translucent at first then growing more opaque and intense. A mist appeared inside the column and through it images arose.

Agnes, peering through the mist, broke the silence. "Are those trees?"

Trace nodded. Through the red haze a landscape had formed. Magenta Trees, Crimson rocks, Maroon bushes all topped by an burgundy sky.

"Pretty Trippy. Looks like a great vacation spot. I wonder if you need sunscreen?" asked Trace.

"It's a portal...perhaps?" Agnes asked quietly.

"Perhaps." Trace retrieved a water bottle from his pack. He tossed it toward the column. It passed the threshold in a burst of bright red light. A few moments later, the water bottle appeared on the ground by a small red bush. Trace stepped forward.

Agnes stopped him. "Where are you going?"

Trace smiled at her. "I want to get my water bottle."

"But we have no idea what might happen to us if we cross into that...thing. Can we get out again? Or will we be trapped in red land forever? I'm not sure about this. Perhaps if we..."

Before she could finish her sentence a gunshot rang out. Agnes suddenly felt a burning sensation in her shoulder as Trace instinctively dived toward her, pushing her forwards into the column. There was a blinding flash of red light and Trace felt for a moment as though he were being turned inside out. Then the sensation passed as he landed with a grunt on the other side of the portal, on top of Agnes.

He looked back at the portal. On this side the portal showed a bright blue dome. Six blue, armed, humans were running towards the portal.

Trace pulled out his gun and fired a few shots towards the portal. The blue humans scattered. One of them went down, blue blood oozing from a wound on his chest.

"Come on we've got to get out of here!"

Trace grabbed Agnes's hand and the two ran away from the portal towards a copse of red trees. They plunged into the cover of the forest and kept moving. Trace spared a glance over his shoulder before the forest swallowed them up. Four red humans were diving out of the portal landing unceremoniously on the ground. A fifth arrived, much more adroitly, and began barking orders at the others. They were looking around confused as to which way Trace and Agnes had gone. Trace turned back to the forest and urged Agnes on, thankful for the escape.

An hour later Trace reached the end of the forest and ran into a wall. Agnes came behind him, breathing hard.

"Why...why did we stop?"

"We seemed to have reached the end of the road." Trace reached out his hand and touched the red wall in front of him. "It appears as though we are in another giant dome. This one Red. I wonder if they come in all the colours. By the way, Red looks good on you. Your hair looks like it's on fire."

Agnes sniffed not sure whether it was a compliment. She sat down on a boulder wincing and clutching her shoulder.

"Here let me have a look at that." Trace leaned over and checked Agnes's shoulder, while she caught her breath.

"Only a graze." He searched through the packs and came up with a small medical kit. "So much for a million miles from nowhere."

"But how did they find us? How?" Agnes asked, wincing as Trace applied a bandage to her wound.

"Doesn't matter, they're here now. Armed and dangerous I suspect the shot wasn't planned, someone got trigger happy."

"So any ideas what to do now?"

Trace looked over the contents of both packs. He handed Agnes a protein bar and a water bottle. "Dinner?" Agnes took the bar and water and watched Trace do inventory.

"We have enough water and delicious food in vacuum packs for a day. So whatever we are supposed to find in Red-ville, we'd better do it quickly. Let's see, 2 guns and ammo, a couple of flares..."

"What are those?" Agnes asked look at two flat metal containers.

"Land mines. Boom Boom." Trace put them aside and from a side pocket retrieved the red stone. It was emitting a low pulsing sound. "Well this is interesting."

Agnes stood up. "Here let me see it. She walked a few paces back into the forest. The pulsating seemed to quicken. She came back to where Trace was waiting. Well that solves where we have to go, the question is how do we get there safely?"

"I suggest we go on the offensive. We need to lead our friends away from where this thing is leading us. I have a plan, but we'll have to move fast and light."

<\>

These humans were easy and predictable, Krynos thought as he watched them do his bidding through their eyes. Vain and obvious were their choices for submission. It was a strange world he had been thrust into, one that he would relish leading with an iron fist. He wasn't happy with his first link, Eddy, he would have preferred someone stronger, but Eddy had finally proven worthwhile in the acquisition of his current chain of men, conditioned to do his bidding.

Once the keys were his, he would destroy his prison forever and the power of the Sourcestone would once again be fully his to master, he would not need these puny humans for anything, except as slaves. Then he would reach out to the stars and exact his revenge on those that imprisoned him and abandoned him. First though he would start with Noth. It was a surprise to him to find a guardian still left on this world, a throwback to another time. A relic. The fight with him had drained him considerably, he would have to be careful, but when he succeeded and the gates of Chaos were opened   he would begin his reign of suffering with Noth. Krynos squelched his excitement and concentrated on his task. Through the eyes of another...

<\>

The voice in Sergeant Vladimir Konstan's head was insistent.

"Keep moving, find them, you will be rewarded."

He pounded the red ground in an organized search pattern as he had been trained to do in special ops, before he had been decommissioned and sent to the reserves. He was pissed about that. Someone had it in for him, for sure. At 6'6" he towered over the others under his command. He was used to using brute force, smashing first with tree club arms or getting in close with the giant buck knife he carried. Guns were a weak man's weapon, but he had one on him-just in case, a 357 magnum capable of punching a hole in a man's head the size of a grapefruit.

Those under him answered to his command immediately. He was not above beating a man into submission for the others to see. His eyes were eagle sharp providing a window into an agile but cruel mind. When the voice first came to him, he had resisted. But after awhile he could not understand why he fought, the voice was so reasonable and it offered benefits.

Energy poured through him. He felt as though he could go for days without food, water or rest. It promised him things also. *Power.* The chance to be back in special ops. Only this time in command over those who had been promoted before him and ultimately pushed him out. All he had to do was follow and capture at least one of the two people they were following and locate some artifact said to be at this locale. The other person was expendable. Sergeant Konstan knew which scenario he would prefer; the red head would look very nice writhing beneath him.

The red environment had caused him only momentary confusion, but he was trained to ignore what was unimportant. After about an hour of mapping out this location, he learned they were in a dome of some kind. Which made his job easier. Using the five men remaining to him he had started at one side of the dome and began a search pattern. He would have liked a few more men, and losing one had been an annoyance: trigger-happy. Blew their perfect ambush. *Yes, Idiots like that were expendable,* Konstan thought.

Guy's name had been 'Colcheck'. Konstan preferred 'Idiot'. He was in the middle of composing an epitaph for 'Idiot' when he saw the flare. He barked an order through his com-set to the others.

"Grid pattern delta. Let's see what that was, but be cautious. I don't want to lose any of you until I have to."

The 'until' would briefly resonate in their minds, but only temporarily. Each of the men had been promised something by the voice of Krynos as he whisked away their resistance like a cobweb, making them see more 'clearly'.

Konstan and his men worked their way over toward where the flare had lit the red sky in a brief amber flash. Konstan was thinking hard as to why his quarry would be so foolish as to fire the flare, unless they had other support. Ever cautious in battle, Konstan thought furiously through the possibilities.

They moved through the wooded section carefully and met up as a team at the dome wall. Konstan continued to fight back questions as to where they were and focused on his prize and its rewards. The men lingered about 20 paces from him waiting for instructions. The two were leading him on a chase, but why?

Konstan didn't like being led around and he ground his teeth in frustration. The red atmosphere in this dome seemed to be dragging his thoughts as though he were thinking through a red fog. Still lost in thought, Konstan watched from a distance as one of his men walked over to an object on the ground and bent down to examine it. It looked like a backpack. Konstan suddenly snapped to attention

"DON'T TOUCH THAT!" He yelled.

Too late. The blast of the explosion rocked the dome. The men closest to the booby trap were blown to pieces, the others injured and unconscious. Konstan was thrown back against a tree, but remained conscious. Surprisingly a flood of energy suddenly poured through him as the voice filled his mind. *"MOVE!"* it screamed at him, *"FIND THEM!"* Konstan was on his feet breathing hard but feeling powerful. He searched the area for about five minutes then picked up a trail heading off into the forest. Konstan felt the giddy flush of the hunter and set off after his prey.

Half an hour after setting the trap, Trace and Agnes heard the distant percussion of the exploding mines. They looked at each other, both silently acknowledging that their actions may have caused the deaths of others; both of them, grimly aware that they had no other choice. Agnes tore her eyes away from Trace and continued to follow the ever-brightening stone in her hand.

"We don't know what might have happened back there, Agnes. If any of them, or all, survived, it won't take long for them to pick up our trail. How much further do you think?"

"I'm not sure...The stone suddenly began to pulsate very quickly as they made their way through a dense section of the red forest."

Suddenly, they popped through the trees into a clearing.

"I think we're there...what is that?"

At the center of a twenty foot round clearing was a triangular stone set on it's point, somehow defying gravity. Above the dais floated an amber rock, brilliant red light flowing out of it washing the entire dome in red.

Trace strode purposefully toward the dais.

"I would say, we have found our keystone. All right let's get it and figure out how to get out of...OW!"

Trace suddenly hit a rock wall full on, his forehead and nose taking the brunt of the damage.

"Are you alright?" Agnes rushed over to his side. Trace had dropped to the ground and was rubbing his face.

"That is going to leave a beautiful bruise. Fortunately I never get bleeding noses."

"Really?"

"Never. In my whole life. And I've been whacked in the nose a few time if you can imagine."

Agnes looked at him and arched her eyebrows. "Yes, I can imagine that." Trace reached out a hand and touched the solid invisible wall in front of him.

"This is the weirdest thing. Feels like a block of stone. Maybe we should have kept one of the mines. Not sure how we are going to blast our way past this."

Agnes reached out her own hand and felt...nothing. In fact her hand moved past where Trace's was and passed through unobstructed.

"How did you do that?"

Agnes held up the small rectangular stone in her hand.

"Seems I've got a key to this place." She stood up and walked through where the barrier was and was inside. She looked back at Trace.

"Well Agnes, seems like you have back stage access. Go get that keystone and let's get the hell out of here."

Agnes nodded and turned. She walked toward the dais, the red glow bathing her in intense light. She felt like she was on fire with no heat. She approached the dais on which the amber stone hovered patiently. *How long*, Agnes wondered, *has it been waiting here? How long ago since Noth had constructed this place?* The Archeologist inside of her began asking questions. If only she had a few days to study all of this...but she didn't have a few days. Agnes reached out toward the stone but stopped at the sound of a cry of pain from behind her. She whirled around to see Trace locked in battle with an enormous bloody man.

"Trace!"

"Agnes! Get the stone get out of here!"

The big man had pinned Trace to the ground. In his hand he held a giant knife. Trace's hands were locked around the man's wrists and the two were locked in a battle of wills. Agnes did not have her gun, it was in the remaining pack outside of the force field. Trace struggled and Agnes knew that as brawny as Trace was, the slab of muscle with the knife was going to win. Through gritted teeth Trace called out again.

"AGNES...GET OUT OF HERE..."

Agnes made her choice. With a cry she bolted and flew toward Trace, launching herself in the last few moments toward Trace's attacker. She saw a flash of anger pass over the big man's face as she crashed into him. The momentum released the men's hands as they rolled over and the knife was knocked free from the man's grip.

Agnes felt her knee connect solidly with the man's face before her momentum carried her over the other side of him. She landed hard and had the breath knocked out of her. She looked up gasping to see the man jump to his feet and cross to Trace. The man swung a club fist to the side of Trace's head has he struggled to get up. Trace dodged the blow and came in to lock his arms under the man's torso, trying to wrestle him to the ground. The man landed a few weak blows to the side of Trace's head in an attempt to break free from his grip.

Agnes acted without thinking. Still trying to regain her breath she crawled quickly over to retrieve the knife that had dropped. The man smacked his hands hard over Trace's ears, causing Trace to let go. The man then kneed Trace in the stomach making him double over. The man was just about to hammer down on Trace's head when Agnes plunged the blade of the big knife into his side. He let out a roar of agony and staggered back.

Agnes took the moment to run past the man and grab Trace's arm. She wasn't sure if what she planned would work but she had to try. Still holding Trace's hand she ran through the barrier surrounding the dais. To her relief both of them plunged through. She looked back to see the man, a grim look of terrible determination on his face, pull the blade out from his side. Ultra red blood began pouring from his red skin. Then with a snarl he ran full tilt toward them only to smack solidly into the barrier.

The man staggered back from the blow, but surprisingly did not get knocked out. With a raging roar he pulled out a big handgun. And began firing at Trace and Agnes. Trace had come to by then and to Agnes's surprise threw himself in front of her. She screamed. The bullets did not enter the force field. The man emptied his gun then hurled it at the barrier in frustration.

Konstan began to scream at the two in a stream of Russian invectives. The pain in his side was awful. He fell to the ground in agony. He knew he was losing a lot of blood and would pass out soon. The voice came to his mind. Another failure. You humans are so weak. When I conquer you, I will crush you all...the voice suddenly left him. Konstan mind reeled at the sudden departure of the voice.

Then Konstan came back to reality. He looked wildly around him. Where was he? The last thing he remembered he was at the reserve office filling in some paper work. He was surrounded by a red forest...he was bleeding and in great pain...was he dreaming? It all felt so real. He looked up to see two people a short distance away standing by a rock reaching for a glowing amber rock. He called out to them...

Agnes turned just as she retrieved the amber rock from its place above the Dais. She heard the big man call out to them. There was fear in his voice. He was crying for help. Their eyes met as her hands wrapped around the stone. The stone dropped into her hand. Then the red world outside the force field disintegrated, like grains of red sand blown into the wind. Terror flooded the man's eyes and Agnes and Trace watched in horror as he too, disintegrated. A muffled cry of confusion and pain was cut off in an instant.

Agnes gasped, "Dear God..."

The sentence was lost as within the force field the dais began to spin. Trace grabbed Agnes as an energy vortex spun from the dais to swallow them. Trace felt like his atoms were being pulled apart. He hung on to Agnes tightly with his thoughts, for his body was scattered into a million pieces. Then there was darkness.

A voice from far away. "Trace? Trace? Can you hear me?"

Heat. He felt heat on his body, which felt like it had hastily been reassembled with a few pieces missing. Was this the mother of all hangovers? Trace wondered. He didn't recall any grappa with the boys or hot women.

"Trace?"

Trace slowly opened his eyes and blinked hard as bright, hot sunlight filled his vision. "Ow"...That fucking hurts." Then a shadow appeared in front of him. Through squinting eyes he made out Agnes's face. His eyes focused more. He was lying flat on his back on hot sand. His memory returned in a flood of unpleasant images. He tried to force them down, as he usually did, with sarcasm.

"Hey there Agnes. Fun ride eh?"

Trace tried to laugh, but it came out sounding like a consumptive cackle. It felt like his lungs were trying to crawl out of his body. Agnes helped him to a sitting position then sat beside him. She was still clutching the amber stone. He looked around and to his amazement, discovered they were sitting all alone in the middle of a desert.

"Nice beach," he said.

Agnes looked miserable. "That was horrible. That man...those men..."

Trace stopped her by reaching out and putting his hand firmly on her shoulder.

"Deserve to be avenged." With an effort, he slowly got to his feet on unsteady legs. "Not quite sure how at this moment in time, but all of those that have been used by Krynos will be avenged."

He looked back at her at met her eyes. A look of steal crossed over her. She nodded once. He nodded back.

"I could use a dip in the pool and a Margueritta. How about you?"

Agnes let out an abortive laugh and shook her head. She got to her feet as a helicopter arrived on the horizon. Trace tensed wondering if it was another attack, knowing there was nowhere to hide. Then, as the chopper got closer, he could see an arm waving from the cockpit. It was the Colonel.

"Oh...great." he said, "Here's our ride."

TEN: Repercussions

Harry felt the sting of the back of Eddy's hand. His head barely moved, but a small trickle of blood oozed from Harry's mouth.

"Look harder!" Eddy screamed at the big man.

They were in Eddy's apartment, trying to search for the whereabouts of Anderson and the woman. Eddy could feel the failure of the last group he had helped to recruit. He was sure that these men would not fail. Well trained, easily corrupted. Eddy couldn't understand it. They were all big men. Strong, without any real moral center.

The biggest one had been the husband of a cousin he used to harass when he was younger. Used to beg her at family functions to show him her breasts. She never did. She would slap him instead and figured out some ingenious ways to humiliate Eddy.

One time, at a birthday party he had walked in on her when she was changing into her bathing suit. She threw a glass at his head, hitting him square on the temple. He had blacked out for a few minutes, when he came to; she was gone to the pool. When he joined the party around the pool, she figured out a way to pants him in front of the whole party. The younger kids shrieked at his dwindling manhood, the older woman chuckled. His Dad turned away in disgust and ordered another beer. This had been his ultimate payback, taking her husband Konstan, and making him a puppet for his use.

But that big fucker had failed. Eddy had failed and soon he would feel Krynos's wrath. He was restoring now, because he had been exerting himself so much. But Krynos would come back stronger than ever, he could feel the charge along the link, even though Krynos was currently dormant; Krynos would be back in full force soon. Not much time then. Eddy had been using Harry's contacts to look for any unusual air traffic around where they had found Anderson and the girl. Harry had proven to be more useful than he had thought he would. The man had some 'habits' that necessitated the use of unchartered flights for the purposing of importing. One lead would save Eddy and placate Krynos.

"Find anything yet, you big fuck?"

"Nothing sir. I have a few more sources to check though." Harry sounded genuinely distressed that he couldn't help Eddy. Eddy was going to strike him again, just for the hell of it, when Krynos woke up.

Unrelenting pain filled Eddy's body. Every nerve, every fiber of his being was a source of pain. There was no escape. Eddy couldn't even cry out, so excruciatingly complete was the agony. One minute Eddy was standing, the next he was on the floor twitching from the torture that Krynos inflicted.

Krynos didn't even speak to Eddy, not even the sound of the torturers voice to provide comfort, just pain. Harry continued to search through his contacts, emails and texts flying off his phone. He hadn't even spared a glance when Eddy went down. He knew, could feel in the link, that he was probably next. Suddenly a text came in. An answer had come through.

"I've got it!" Harry screamed out in joyous triumph.

The pain in Eddy ceased immediately, the sudden removal of the pain caused him to gasp, then it started again, slightly less intense than before.

Harry repeated himself, yelling even louder than before. "I've got it! I think I know where they went!" Eddy had heard Harry also. Through clenched teeth he spoke through the pain in a hoarse whisper. "Krynos, please stop, I found them. Please..."

The pain continued for a moment more, rising to peak intensity then stopping altogether. Eddy's ears were ringing.

"WHERE ARE THEY?" Krynos's voice reverberated in Eddy's head. *"SPEAK!"*

"Harry, quickly...tell him!" Eddy croaked.

Harry began to babble. "I have this contact in the coast guard who knows of an independent operator who..."

"WHERE ARE THEY!!!?"

The mental shout caused both men to scream out in pain. Harry detailed the whereabouts, location and direction of an unidentified helicopter about a hundred miles from the place they had dropped Konstan and his men. The helicopter had been tracked to a small nearby port, mostly abandoned.

"SHOW ME."

Harry punched up a satelite picture of the area. Through Harry's eyes Krynos saw.

"I KNOW THIS PLACE. SO LONG AGO. I KNOW THIS PLACE."

There was silence in the minds of both Eddy and Harry for a long time. Eddy managed to get off the floor; Harry sat mute and hopeful in front of the computer. Then Krynos came back.   *"YOU HAVE BOTH SERVED...POORLY."*

Both men cringed at their failure.

"EDDY!"

"Yes, my...lord?" Eddy's voice was a mere whisper.

"YOU WILL GO TO THIS PLACE. I MUST BE CLOSER! I CANNOT DO WHAT I WANT TO DO FROM HERE. YOU WILL GO THERE NOW! HARRY WILL ARRANGE IT...WON'T YOU HARRY?"

The voice was more soothing for Harry, who nodded his head stupidly, much like an over praised dog.

"Eddy..."

The voice had stopped screaming and was now tinged with seduction.

"Eddy, when Harry is done, you will take care of Harry won't you?"

Eddy looked over at Harry and realized the big man could not hear Krynos's voice in that moment. Nor could Harry see the beautiful image Krynos place in Eddy's mind of Eddy bashing Harry's brains out with the bat he kept by the door. Eddy salivated and whimpered. When he spoke, his voice was a reverent whisper.

"Yes, My Lord."

ELEVEN: Out To Sea

Eddy hated to travel, especially by plane. He had Harry get him a private flight to intercept Anderson and the woman. Then he had bashed Harry's head in. Eddy wasn't a violent man by nature, but every blow had made him feel better and more energized with Krynos's guidance that quelled the tiny voice a million miles away inside of him that was quaking at the horror of his actions.

Before the end, Harry's eyes had changed. He looked like he had awakened from a dream into a nightmare. Harry had opened his mouth to speak but Krynos had guided Eddy's last blow to finish him off. Then a wave of intense pleasure had flooded Eddy's body making him groan in ecstasy.

Now he was flying. A curvy brunette with big doe eyes had offered him a drink, bending over him, her pendular breasts swinging near his face. Eddy could feel his meager hard-on pressing against his pants. Sure he would take her in the air and show her how a real man fucked. Take her in a thousand different ways. Eddy licked his lips as she fussed with his tray. Then the plane banked left. Eddy puked all over her. She had disappeared after that and Eddy only saw her on his way out, a plastic smile plastered to her face, wearing an oversized man's suit.

Finding Anderson and the girl had been relatively easy. The fishing port was relatively small and two strangers stuck out like a sore thumb. A few well-placed questions placed them at a small house on the outskirts of town. They stayed there for an entire day, never leaving, probably resting up after their adventures in the jungle.

They finally left late in the afternoon on the following day. Eddy trailed them through the meager village market, despondent sellers hawking t-shirts and fake watches to the odd tourist. Food vendors sweltering in the heat of the sun pushing food they could; fried, re-fried, or deep-fried.

The smell of oily food and unwashed bodies assaulted Eddy's delicate nose has he nipped and tucked his way around stalls, keeping a safe distance from Anderson and the girl. Watching. Both were grim faced and barely talked as they bought some shriveled fruit from a stall. Eddy noticed how many times Anderson looked over at the woman, drinking her in with his big bastard eyes. Disgusting pig. Like he had a chance with a piece like that. Eddy's eyes trailed over her body, nicely curvy with a perfect ass and a long throat. Eddy liked long throats, could imagine his tongue exploring every crevice, her moaning in ecstasy over Eddy's touch. *FOCUS!* Krynos's voice slapped his mind and Eddy winced, fighting to keep from crying out.

The fat, old man vendor at the shirt stall he was pretending to look over gave him a funny look, then turned back to another customer. He regained his composure in time to see the pair move off down the street. Eddy hurried to follow, Kryno's admonition still ringing in his mind.

"REMEMBER THEY KNOW YOU, YOU CANNOT BE SEEN...IMBECILE."

He followed them discreetly most of the day. Krynos fed him with energy, making his movements lythe and his mind sharp. It was like twenty cups of coffee without the jitters. He watched the two now speaking to a local scuba for hire boat captain. Eddy got in close so he could hear the exchange.

"...My wife and I want to explore the reef off the coast."

"Do you have much experience?" The captain asked

The pair answered at once. "No. Yes."

Anderson rolled his eyes. "Don't worry dear. I have lots of experience. This is our honeymoon, remember?"

Through clenched teeth, Argwhistle answered.

"Yes...you're right...dear. You will show me the way and guide me as you always do."

The captain smiled. "Your choice, of course, I could guide you, but if you prefer your husband that is no problem. I will wait topside for you. It is too late in the day, today, though...shall we say the morning?"

Argwhistle looked disappointed. "Uh...sure, if you think that is best. It is late...if someone hadn't slept so long..." She made an accusing sweep with her eyes toward Anderson.

Anderson laughed in an awkward way while elbowing the captain. "Well it is our honeymoon, after all." Fake laughs all around. *Dear God!* This was the worst acting Eddy had ever seen. He shook his head in disgust, and then ducked behind a shed while Anderson and Argwhistle headed away.

Eddy turned his attention back to the captain who had set about coiling a length of rope on the dock. A lithe, leathery-skinned man with a big face that had spent most of its time outdoors, the sun having erased the man's exact race years ago. He looked capable and strong. Eddy chuckled softly to himself and felt a surge of energy from Krynos as he moved toward the man. No problem. Capturing this one's soul should be a piece of cake.

<></>

Trace loved the water. Could spend endless hours in it. Craved it when he was away from it. Getting up early with Agnes to slosh around underwater, looking for some ancient artifact while the distinct possibility of getting killed hung over their heads, put a bit of a damper on the whole event, however. The pair had a quick breakfast, silent and awkward, the two of them, out on the porch of the little house the Colonel had found for this stage of their quest. The Colonel had said it belonged to an old friend but didn't elaborate more.

Agnes hadn't said more than a fistful of words to Trace over the past couple of days. She had withdrawn, all turtle like, into her beautiful shell. No amount of his inane babbling could rouse her out of her funk, so he left her alone. He figured she needed some time to sort through the shock of red bodies disintegrating and all that. Trace had to admit that he was probably in shock also, but was too stubborn to admit it. Does one really know when one is in shock? Maybe that was the problem. He did know that it was shocking how much he wanted her to get pissed at him...hell anything besides the sullen silence that existed between them.

Trace wondered to himself where Chaos ended and order began. When he looked back at a series of seemingly random events, he always ordered them along a cause and effect timeline. Trace believed humans liked it that way. They are uncomfortable with seeing time as anything more than a direct line.

Trace saw it differently, however. He believed the past, present and future existed simultaneously in order to create experience. *We are alone, locked in our little shell bodies and the notion of chaos is terrifying to us.* Time is merely a convenient way for us to logically order our days to structure the chaos, but is it really necessary to do so in order to fully appreciate our experience of life, to understand our lives?

He found it kind of depressing actually. He read obituaries that were so concerned with the timeline, the narrative of the deceased. 'He was born in Yonkers to loving hardworking parents then went on to University where he discovered a new formula for squeeze cheese. Then, after University he formed a company. Then he met and married Lindsay and then he had four children, and then and then and then."

Trace preferred the Chaos and shunned the organization of it all. *Does Agnes care about me? Or am I reliving a fantasy of the unobtainable woman I had met in my early twenties? Do I care about her or am I drugged on hormones and desire? Does it really matter? Does the past really inform the present or is it the other way around? Or is the future the thing informing the present?*

While he was setting the booby trap for the bad guys in the jungle, he was remembering three occurrences in his life simultaneously: being a little kid and his Dad catching him burning ants with a magnifying glass. He had lectured Trace about the preciousness of life and about wanton destruction. He was also reliving a car accident that almost took his life and waking up in the hospital to the anxious look of his mother, her face full of tears that he had come back from somewhere. Finally, Trace was remembering the time he got in a fight with a 'friend' who had stolen some camera equipment from him. Trace had found his camera stuff in his friend's apartment and lost it on him in a fistfight.

All three of these memories flashed through him as he set his trap. But his future survival while setting the traps also came into play. Regardless of his experiences in the past, or perhaps because of them, the present was informed by his present need for he and Agnes's future survival.

Trace shook his head to clear his thoughts. Pretty heady stuff for the morning, he had to admit. The idea that people were a chaotic collection of experiences that stayed with them regardless of time disturbed him. Somehow he couldn't help but shake the very human need to make sense of all the craziness of life. It seemed soothing and comforting, especially right now; he was drawn to order the chaos, as all humans seem to need to do, eventually.

Breakfast done, Agnes and Trace cleaned the dishes and packed them away and made the beds for some future guest. They packed their gear and headed out into the flawless morning.

The two trudged their way down the road through the waking town toward the water.

"I'm sorry. He said walking more slowly.

"For what?"

"Well, it's just one of those British things"

"British things?"

"Yeah, well my mother was British and she would say sorry a lot. Even when she wasn't sorry."

"So are you?"

"Am I what? British?"

"Sorry, dumbass."

"Well yes, I guess..."

Agnes stopped walking and rounded on him. "And for what exactly? You know, Anderson I'm a big girl. I can sort through my shit all on my own. Just give me some space will you? I don't need your sorry ass quasi-English apologies. I went into this thing by my own choice. You are not responsible. Let's just get this fucking Keystone and get out of here."

Agnes continued down the road with Trace beside her. He could feel her presence both surround him and invade him. A million thoughts and memories all fought to keep up with what was happening in that moment. His desire represented the future, his silence the past...what the hell then was the present?

He walked along beside her, feeling the uneven pavement beneath his boots, absorbing her tirade.

"Thank you." He said after the silence.

"What the hell for? Is this another British thing?"

"No, nothing really."

He stopped then and so did she. He smiled at her. She just stared at him. Honestly, Trace didn't know what was making him so happy at this moment, considering how unpleasant she had just been. There was something about her that just made him smile.

She stopped and looked up into his face, searching. "What now? Why are you smiling?"

Quick as a thought, Trace stepped over to her, wrapped his hand around her head, and kissed her. Their mouths met with perfect precision, a small muffled cry escaped her throat. Or perhaps it was his. He was not sure. Her mouth yielded to his for a perfect moment and he could feel his own yearning body aching for hers, wanting her.

A few blissful moments later, however, he decided not to press his advantage. Diving in for movie kisses was not normal for him. He reluctantly pulled away from her and looked her full in the eyes, searching for a reaction. She seemed stunned, standing there, rooted to the spot holding a bag containing scuba equipment in the middle of a strange town. After several heartbeats she muttered softly.

"We have to go."

She turned then and strode away from him. He watched her go for a moment, and then hurried to catch up.

Trace and Agnes arrived at the dock at around eight in the morning. The water was like a piece of glass. Captain Terrance was there to greet them. *Guy looks like shit,* Trace thought. *Must have been on a bender last night.* The Captain smiled regardless and within minutes their gear was stowed and the three were flying across the inlet toward open water.

The Colonel had given us the coordinates where we would find the keystone. Trace reminded the Captain of our destination. He nodded quietly without turning.

"Pretty far out" He said after a long while. "Deep waters. Should take about half an hour."

Trace was surprised he didn't talk us into a shallower reef; considering they were supposed to be honeymooners and Agnes had let slip that she was a beginner. Trace didn't think much of it and went back to tell Agnes.

They approached the coordinates and the Captain stopped the boat, working efficiently to weigh anchor and prepare his passengers for the dive. They were about a hundred feet from a series of massive rock formations thrusting skyward from the ocean. The rocks towered over them like giant, twisted gargoyles that had risen from the waters only to be suddenly petrified; frozen in angry surprise. They were barren of any wildlife, worn smooth by years of battling the elements. There was nothing pleasant about them at all.

Trace had to admit that Agnes looked pretty hot snapped into a neoprene wetsuit. The nearness of her left him distracted. She hadn't said much to him since he'd kissed her, *Probably plotting my death.*

He looked over into the dark blue water and thought of a few ways she could off him down there. Once in his gear, Trace plunged into the water and appreciated the coolness to sharpen his thoughts and focus him on the task at hand. The captain had provided them with a couple of cool scuba scooters to propel them underwater. Trace had done a fair amount of diving, mostly in Australia when he was there on a job. Absolutely loved it. Agnes made it into the water with a less than graceful plop, sort of like watching a drunk fall off a deck chair. Trace averted his eyes and checked his mirth as they went under.

Once underneath, Agnes pulled out another rectangular bar, like the one they had used to locate the first keystone. This one, however, pulsed a dull yellow. After getting their bearings they followed its pulsations into the lower depths.

<><>

The captain watched the pair as they descended losing sight of them a few feet under. A monumental fight was going on inside of him. A part of him wanted to shout at them, to warn them. But the presence was there, tearing at his resolve, forcing him mute. After the pair disappeared, the voice came to him again. He had spent the entire night fighting its seductive urgings. He had resisted, but an energy force had seized control of him and forced him to do it's bidding.

The captain knew the two were in danger, from what, he wasn't sure, but was helpless to lend aid. In the end, he had become a reluctant puppet, going through the motions, watching himself from afar as his body was directed by the presence inside of him. *"WE MUST BE CLOSER. MOVE."* The captain made a weak gesture of defiance but was rewarded with a blinding flash of pain. It soon subsided as the power began to move him. He stood up and set about putting his gear on, he had no control, could only watch his body go through the motions. Within minutes he was slipping into the water after Trace and Agnes.

Agnes made her way down through the depths following Trace, her underwater scooter propelling her with ease. She had to admit she quite liked being able to breathe underwater. She had done a lot of snorkeling when she was a teenager and was a strong swimmer, but this was a new whole world opening up to her. The water was so clear; it felt like she was flying over the vast underwater landscape. Vibrant colours and small exotic fish made her feel like she was in an animated film and for a moment she forgot what she was down here for, allowing herself to feel the exhilaration of a new experience. *Kind of like Trace's kiss this morning.*

The scene crashed into her reverie like a hammer. It was so unexpected, that kiss, but not forced. *Warm and tender and....enveloping.* In that moment, Agnes could feel her self-control slipping and when the kiss was over and he was looking at her...into her...she felt for a moment, lost. Then reality had flooded over her and her warring emotions left her in a state of deadlock.

What was she doing? That felt so good. We have a job to do. Our lives had been threatened. All those men, dead. When Trace had looked at her, she saw him disintegrating like the man in the red dome. *NO!* She had turned away then, in that moment of a thousand thoughts, there was little else she could do. Agnes liked to be in control. She was an Aries, after all.

Agnes and Trace were drawn deeper into the water's depths. The base of the rock formation they had anchored off above loomed large in front of them. The stone rectangle pulsated ever more strongly in Trace's hand the closer they got. Trace searched the surfaces for some sign of the keystone or where they were supposed to go. There was nothing but solid rock, yet the rectangle urged them on.

Finally, they reached the rock face and Trace and Agnes spent some time examining the rough rock before they found the keyhole. Strangely uniform, it was surprising to Trace that he hadn't noticed it right away. It was only for the rectangle rock whose pulsations grew rapid then changed to a solid colour when the keyhole came into view. Trace looked back at Agnes and shrugged, a difficult task with two air tanks on your back. He placed the rectangle into the hole and a large portion of the rock simply disappeared in a blinding flash of yellow light. Deja vu, Trace thought as he entered a yellow dome, many times the size of the blue one back in the jungle.

The captain held back, making sure he wasn't seen. He watched, confused, as Agnes and Trace approached the rock wall, then couldn't believe his eyes as the rock disappeared and yellow light poured from the opening. .

"THAT IS FAR ENOUGH!"

The captain winced as the voice boomed in his head. He stopped suddenly, forcing himself to slow his breathing, then he felt himself filling with energy, a presence began to form inside of him. It was Krynos, inhabiting him, forcefully taking him over. The Captain felt like he was being crammed into one corner of himself as a squatter took over his internal space. It was a decidedly uncomfortable feeling; he felt as though he were going to burst as Krynos's presence grew. Just as it grew unbearable, the energy shot out of his body, draining him, leaving only a thin tether behind, still in control. From some corner of his being he wondered what had just happened. He felt used and exhausted, the tether to Krynos the only thing keeping him alive and conscious, otherwise he would have simply given up and gone to sleep.

"NO SLEEP FOR YOU, HUMAN. YOU WILL MAINTAIN A WATCH UNTIL I RETURN."

The voice came and went in an instant, leaving the Captain with a feeling of trapped despair. He floated above the cave entrance wondering what would happen next. A short while later, movement from his left drew his attention, a drifting shadow in the distance growing larger. The Captain started to panic looking around for someplace to hide.

"CALM."

The voice came and went in an instant leaving him suddenly relaxed, more than relaxed- mutely paralyzed would be more accurate. The shadow grew closer and within a few heartbeats, The Captain made out the form of an enormous creature, something out of nightmare. As big as a transport truck, the head was craggy and covered in spikes, deep, black, sunken eye sockets. The mouth a broad and angry vertical slash. The body was vast, tentacled and squid-like. It moved toward the Captain with a grace that belied its size, deep, dark eyes searching. The Captain recoiled in his soul; this was not a creature of the sea, more like one from the depths of Hades itself.

What in hell is that? The Captain recoiled in horror and fought to regain control from Krynos. Krynos's presence, soothed and promised and stroked him from the inside and he felt himself relax as though he were drugged.

"Don't fear, Captain. There are a very small number of creatures of your planet that still exist from the time of my race's occupation of Earth. You create myths around them; many are skeptical of their existence; yet they are real. My race brought these creatures to your planet many thousands of years ago, their DNA is compatible to my power; I can influence it, through you, to achieve our goals. You want to achieve our goals, do you not, Captain?"

Reluctantly the captain felt his head nod inside his mask. The voice continued to calm. *"You are a powerful link, Captain, and I will reward you for your bravery and service to me."*

More pleasure coursed through the Captain images of financial freedom for his struggling wife and children, quieting the rebellious voice inside him that screamed at him to resist and fight back.

The Captain shook his head, resolved to help his family at all costs. He moved back from the entrance as the creature came closer. He wasn't quite sure how it was going to fit through such a small hole, then watched in fascinated horror as the creature reached through the entrance with one of its tentacles while the rest of its body...stretched.

Before his eyes the creature became incredibly long like a fleshy rope of flesh, then it disappeared through the entrance like it was being sucked through a straw. In a moment it was gone. The Captain stayed outside the entrance and waited.

Oblivious that they had now become prey, Trace and Agnes explored the watery dome, intense yellow light refracting through the water in an unsettling way. Trace felt like he was in a giant cup of urine. They followed the light as it intensified going higher. Within moments, they had surfaced inside the sphere, in the center of which, suspended by an unseen force, and hovered the keystone. Trace took out his mouthpiece and tested for air, taking a breath. Satisfied, he nodded to Agnes to remove hers.

"Now what? How are we supposed to get at that? Maybe we could chuck something at it."

Agnes rolled her eyes.

"Stop rolling your eyes at me, unless you have a better suggestion?" He looked over at her, infused by the light of the dome. "By the way, yellow is NOT your colour."

"Not flattering on you either, pee-man. My suggestion is: investigate first, chuck stuff at it later."

Agnes drifted toward the center of the chamber underneath where the keystone was suspended, about thirty feet above. She pulled out the rectangular key she had retrieved when the dome door had opened. It had become translucent and when she looked into the depths of the stone a bright yellow light was beginning to form. It began to swirl, and then grow in size, until it left the stone and was surrounding her. The water around her began to stir quietly until it spinning. Agnes could feel herself being lifted on a swirling column of water, up toward the hovering keystone. It was a giddy experience, one that made her laugh out loud, like some crazy ride at a water park.

Trace watched, transfixed, as Agnes was elevated. He found himself smiling along with her, watching as her smile transformed her yellow face into something beyond beautiful. *No, I don't regret kissing her.*

After a few moments the column stopped rising and Agnes reached out her hands and retrieved the keystone. As she did so, the water began to descend toward the water, once again. Trace cheered as Agnes looked over him and shook the keystone in the air like a triumphant trophy. Just as she was reaching the water level again, an enormous tentacle flew out of the water, wrapped itself around Agnes and the keystone and pulled her down into the depths below.

It happened so fast; Trace barely had time to register what he was seeing. He screamed out "Agnes!" but she was gone in an instant.

His heart hammering in his chest, Trace quickly put his mouthpiece and goggles back on and dove beneath the water. The sight before him stunned Trace. A sea monster of epic proportions filled the chamber. Clutched in its tentacles was Agnes, struggling against its hold. She had managed to get her mouthpiece back on, but her goggles were nowhere to be seen, she was fighting almost blind beneath the water.

Trace jumped into action. He swam toward the tentacle that held Agnes, but was caught by another around his lower legs. The pressure was intense. Trace pulled out his knife and began to hack at the creature's flesh. It was like armor. He raised the knife high over his head and plunged it down into the tentacle. Piercing through flesh, the tentacle quivered for a moment then squeezed tighter, pulling Trace toward the gaping maw in the middle of its head. Trace stared in horror at the abyss of the mouth and fought frantically for release. *No way I'm going to be fish food today,* he thought. An idea formed in his mind, risky and doomed for failure, but his choices were limited.

Reaching to his waist, he released the straps that held his oxygen tanks. They began to float free as he worked his shoulders out of the straps. The mouth got closer. Trace spared a look over at Agnes, who appeared to have passed out, she was being shaken like a rag doll, but her grip remained locked around the keystone. Trace reached to his waist and removed the diving weights he had strapped on. He could barely feel his legs as the tentacle stopped the flow of blood to them.

Working furiously, he attached the belt of weights to the tanks by the strap, took a few deep breaths on the regulator then dropped it toward the grisly mouth before him. The tanks fell quickly down toward the creature. Trace pulled out his Glock and prepared to fire. He knew that he might have one shot before the gun likely blew up in his hand, if it worked at all; there were no guarantees underwater with a gun. But he knew it could be done. The sound waves might even make him deaf, if the shock waves didn't rip out his organs. *So many fun ways to die.*

Trace raised the gun and took aim, as if the gun might work properly. The tank dropped through the mouth opening. Trace fired. The shockwave from the explosion that ensued blew Trace clear of the creature, somehow the tentacle that held him buffering the explosion in his favor. He whirled through the water and felt the embrace of oblivion envelope him, Trace fought it, and thrashing wildly in the violent eddies caused by the blast. Bits of creature littered the water around him. His lungs were screaming for air. His left leg seemed to have gone completely numb. *Get topside,* his only thought. With every ounce of energy he had left he kicked with his right leg toward the water's surface.

Trace emerged and gasped for air to quell his screaming lungs. The chamber had gone dark, somehow damaged by the explosion. A dim light was playing on the surface of the water nearby. Trace could barely think, so muddled was his head. He certainly couldn't hear anything, the shock wave having destroyed his hearing. Was it permanent? Trace didn't have time to worry about it as he swam toward the light.

A shape appeared bobbing in the water before him. At first he thought it was a piece of monster, but soon realized it was the unmoving form of Agnes. She was lying on her back covered in blood, buoyed up by her air tanks, a small emergency light flickering in the murky water.

With a cry he couldn't hear, Trace swam over to her.

Agnes was alive, though her breathing was ragged. In the water he couldn't tell exactly where the wound was. He had to get her out of here fast. To his surprise, Agnes still held on to the keystone. Somehow, her last conscious thought must have been to hold on. Trace's regulator was still attached to his suit. He retrieved it and worked for what seemed an eternity to rig it up to one of Agnes's tanks and transfer her weights over to him. He would have to work hard to get her back under the water and out of the dome, then topside. He wasn't even sure if there was enough oxygen for the journey, but again, choice in the matter was dictated by need.

Making sure Agnes was still breathing, he placed his arm around her and kicked and stroked with all his might toward the chamber's door. Agnes's breathing was becoming more ragged and Trace was spent by the time he reached the door. Trace managed to get her out the door; freedom was so close.

Then he came face to face with the Captain.

Through the mask, Trace saw the hostility in the Captain's eyes as he hovered before him, just before pulling out an ugly looking knife and lunging toward Trace. Trace did his best to dodge the blow, but was rewarded with a deep cut on his arm. He had released Agnes, who, without the diving weights to hold her down, began to drift upwards. The Captain spared a quick glance at her diminishing body then turned his attentions back to Trace. He lunged toward Trace, knife held for a killing plunge into his heart. Again, Trace was locked in a knife battle; he reached for the Captain's wrist to stop the blow from reaching him. They strained against each other for what seemed an eternity.

Trace looked into the Captain's eyes and saw an epic battle playing out within its depths. The captain seemed to be fighting both Trace and some intense internal battle. The Captains eyes rolled back in his head as he thrashed in Trace's grip. Then he met Trace's eyes again and, for a moment, sanity returned. The Captain looked at Trace, exhaustion and horror playing over his face. Fighting with everything he had, the Captain ceased struggling with Trace, releasing his hands for a moment, then reversing the knife so the blade pointed in his direction. The Captain struggled on and Trace could see he was losing. The last rational thing that the Captain did was nod at Trace, his eyes imploring. At the moment his eyes glazed over and the hostility began to return, Trace plunged the knife deep into the Captain's chest, killing him instantly.

Agnes came to on the boat. She opened her eyes to see Trace looking down at her, his face etched in worry. Her body felt like it had been through a thrashing machine, her head throbbing. It took her a moment to remember what had happened to her, and then it all came back in a rush of horror-film images. It was all so furiously quick the order seemed jumbled: The sea creature, the keystone, being crushed, a dark presence probing her mind, an percussive explosion, blackness. She moaned quietly.

"Agnes?" Trace's voice spoke to her, gentle, concerned. "You okay?"

"I feel like someone hammered on me with a Volkswagen bus."

"Pretty close to the truth, I'd say."

Agnes struggled to a sitting position with Trace's help. The world spun and for a moment she thought she was either going to pass out again, or throw up. She willed herself to do neither. Her torso and her head had been expertly bandaged up, but Agnes could feel that the wounds beneath would take some time healing.

"The Captain?"

Trace got silent for a moment, his jaw tightened. "He...didn't make it."

Agnes decided not to pursue the matter for now. It was then she noticed his condition. "Are you okay?"

"I'll be fine."

One of women's favourite statements made by men. "Okay...I..."

At that moment Agnes suddenly remembered something. She looked down at her hands, expecting it to be there. Her hands were empty; she could feel panic begin to rise inside of her as she started to look wildly around her. She looked at Trace who smiled at her, then reached behind his back, pulling out the Keystone

"Hey, dere Lady, choo lookin' for dis?"

He brought his hands forward. In them was the second keystone. His smile diminished as he looked down at the ancient artifact. "Two down..."

"One to go..."

TWELVE: Evil Re-groups

Eddy was delighted and terrified all at the same time. Delighted that this time it wasn't his fault that they had failed to get yet another keystone. Terrified that it would matter whether it was his fault or not. He would feel the brunt of Krynos's displeasure. He knew that the mission had been unsuccessful, could feel it through the link without knowing the details. Failure had a particular taste that made Eddy's mouth go dry with fear.

He sat in the only bar in town, gulping down toxic 90 proof swill water, in order to numb himself for the ensuing pain. Staggering out into the late afternoon sun, Eddy hoped that perhaps he would simply pass out and at least delay the inevitable. But such was not meant to be.

Krynos's voice came to him intense and low. A shot of energy and he was instantly sober making him sweat with dread. But, to Eddy's surprise, there was no pain. Krynos's presence seemed somewhat subdued as though seen from a distance through a haze. The voice seemed tired, but Eddy knew enough to speak only when he had been spoken to.

"You must go now Eddy, there is still work to do."

No mention of what went on underwater. Only the flash of images and orders given. Then Krynos left him. Not entirely, never entirely, but enough so that Eddy could enjoy a moment of relief. He thought of going in and getting drunk all over again, but no. He would need all his wits for this next assignment. If he failed, all would be lost...at least that is what he thought. He'd been known to be wrong. From time to time.

THIRTEEN: Mountain Momma

Agnes and Trace left in the night. The Colonel had arranged for a seaplane to pick them up. He had also dealt with covering up the loss of the Captain. How, Trace wasn't sure. He didn't bother asking questions, simply packed up his meager belongings and helped Agnes climb aboard. They were moving very slowly, exhaustion and injury catching up to them. Within a few minutes after takeoff they were both fast asleep. They traveled through the night, stopping only briefly to refuel, get something to eat, and then they were back in the air. By the time they landed the following morning, Trace thought he would never get the sound of engines out of his head.

Agnes seemed to have retreated back inside of herself. Trace didn't try to interfere, just spoke as gently as possible to her and only when it was needed. The plane dropped them on a private, frozen airstrip, in the middle of nowhere, someplace surrounded entirely by majestic mountains. Three snowmobiles were waiting for them nearby. Two were empty; on the third was the unmistakable form of the Colonel. He waved his arm in greeting and haled them over. Trace was amazed at the resilience of the old war-horse. Not to mention how connected he was. He had to remember that the next time he was doing a little espionage. The Colonel removed his hat.

"Well hello again young people. I trust you had a pleasant flight?"

Trace sighed and shook the Colonel's hand. He noticed in that moment how old he looked; clearly this was more taxing than the Colonel let on. He couldn't help but think of his father in the home. Still standing as military straight as his body would allow in his fight against gravity and time.

Trace shook his head as a wave of melancholy washed over him.

Trace forced himself to smile and lighten up. "There was no in-flight movie, and certainly no booze. Plus, I don't think I can claim any frequent flyer points. And Agnes's snoring...not sounds that belong to a human being."

They both looked across to Agnes who smiled wanly a she leaned in for a brief hug.   "Hello Colonel. Thank you for everything so far. She looked around at the vast, forbidding mountains before her. So this is where Noth has sent us next, huh? Too much to hope that it is inside a 5 star hotel, huh?"

The Colonel's smile did not reach his eyes. "I'm afraid so, my dear. But you have company this time. I'm coming along with you."

Trace was pleasantly surprised by the addition to their company. The Colonel then offered to go instead of Agnes, but she steadfastly refused.

"I want to see this through...to the end." She said.

Trace was a little turned-on by her fortitude, but he decided against a smart-assed comment.

"Plus," Agnes added, "We still have one of these left."

Agnes held up the last glowing guide stone, this one blue, then handed it over to Trace.

"Me? Why do I get the honors?"

"Noth said this one was keyed to you. Only you can use this one."

 Trace turned the rectangular rock over in his hand. Identical to the others, with one difference: this one glowed blue.

"Okay, guess I'm leading. Let's saddle up and get this over with. Somewhere in the world is a cold beer with my name on it, and I would like to get to it sooner than later."

The Colonel laughed and the three mounted the snowmobiles and whisked off toward the mountains that kept sentry over a 5000 year secret.

They traveled for an hour, the rocky giants growing in size until they dwarfed the three humans. Trace led the way occasionally checking the Guidestone and making adjustments in their course. At length, they came to the base of one of the mountains. This one was not more than remarkable than its brothers around him, and it was certainly as big. The peak lost somewhere in the clouds above. Trace couldn't fathom what they were supposed to do as they reached the base and dismounted. He looked over at the Colonel who was unloading some climbing equipment.

"Whoa! Hold on there old man, you mean we are climbing this monster?" Trace said.

The Colonel just shrugged. "Not really sure, but I like to come prepared. I guess we are waiting on your magic rock to give us the answers."

Trace pulled the stone out of his pocket. Like the others, its pulsations had grown stronger as they approached the mountain. Trace held it up and walked around for a bit getting a heading. When the pulsations seemed to increase he continued in that direction. The others followed as they hiked up a low rock hill that lead to a sheer cliff face.

There. Trace slowed down as he examined its surface. The stones pulsations had stopped, just like all the others. Trace turned to the wall and spotted the keyhole. He looked back at the others.

"Okay, here we go again, at least there won't be any sea monsters here." *Hopefully no monsters at all.*

He placed the key in the slot. A bright blue light shot out from it and a doorway appeared where before there was solid rock. They stepped inside and found yet another dome like the others, only this one did not have a ceiling. Instead, a staircase spiraled up into the darkness above.

"Someone want to look for an elevator?" Trace quipped.

The others looked grim.

"Okay, well let's become stair masters." Trace could only imagine how long this was going to take. The Colonel had supplied them with packs and warm gear, which they received on the plane. He shouldered it now and led the way up the stairs.

The steps were slick and icy, but perfectly formed, not made out of the rock at all. Trace couldn't fathom how it would have been possible to hollow out this mountain, and then place a staircase in the center of it. Another question for Noth. The Colonel had stopped almost immediately and suggested they rope off to each other, in case one should fall. In a matter of moments, his expert hands had them all hitched together and they were on their way once again.

For forty minutes the three trudged around and up the spiral stairs. Agnes was feeling ill from going in circles like this. Her side ached with a dull throb, which had progressively got worse as they climbed. She was out of breath and wasn't quite sure if she had the strength to make it to the top. But she would not give up. She was determined to dig deep for the others that had died on this ridiculous adventure. In a million years she could never have dreamed of such a story. The fact that it actually happened, was happening, did not make it seem more real.

She moved in a daze. The stairs were narrow and slippery and Agnes had to concentrate with everything she had to put one foot in front of another. One slip and the drop into the dark abyss beneath would not be pleasant. She was about to call for a brief rest when Trace stopped up ahead. Agnes and the Colonel made up the intervening steps to stand behind Trace. He was looking ahead of him.

"Why have we stopped?" She said.

"Well, Agnes. Seems we've run out of stairs." Trace said.

Agnes peered around him and saw that, indeed, the steps had stopped rising. Ahead of them was a very narrow strip of the unnatural rock. A pathway that lead into the darkness. It was a bridge to somewhere; a narrow strip of rock, with a sheer drop on both sides. Agnes tried to use her flashlight to see into the gloom, but was only rewarded with more gloom. The thought of crossing it made her nauseous. The three thought together in silence.

Trace broke the silence with a sigh.

"Okay, well the first part of the tour was a bit of a bust, perhaps we can get some good holiday pics from wherever this leads."

Despite herself, Agnes secreted a smile. She didn't want to admit that Trace had a knack of lifting one's spirits with his childish humor, but it did. She certainly didn't let it show to him, so she scowled instead, which seemed to encourage him more, win-win for her.

"Lead on MacDuff..." She said.

Trace re-adjusted the pack on his back. "Hey! No quoting the Scottish play in here, don't you know that it's bad luck?"

The Colonel and her exchanged a glance. She looked back at Trace. "You mean quoting Macbeth...?"

"STOP! Just saying his name can lead to bad luck. And believe me, we've already had enough. Right Colonel?"

The Colonel shook his head looking very tired. He muttered something Agnes didn't hear then spoke up. "I don't know what the fuck either of you are talking about. Let's get going, okay?"

Chastened, Trace shrugged and stepped onto the pathway. The other two followed, a few feet of rope between them. Agnes willed herself to look ahead; the darkness and fatigue were making her light headed. The path was slick and smooth like the stairs, making her cautious with her footing. She took her eyes off Trace for a moment and felt her head whirl.

A steadying hand from the Colonel behind brought her brain back into focus. She breathed deeply and continued on with a quiet thanks. Ten minutes in and the path opened up onto a large stone disk about 12 feet in diameter. The three took a few moments to cautiously explore the sides. It seemed there was no way forward.

Trace walked to the center of the disk, his flashlight playing off the surface.

"What now?" His voice echoed throughout the cavern. "Should we wait for a space ship or something?"

He flapped his hands helplessly into the air. Agnes noticed he sounded a little more annoyed than usual.

"Wait until I get my hands on Noth, couldn't just bury the fucking keystone in a hole, could he...oh no, had to impress us with all this...shit."

Trace's tantrum bounced off the walls, his voice multiplying so that he sounded like a whole room full of boys having a meltdown. Agnes and the Colonel simply watched, feeling helpless.

"I'm not kidding you guys, Noth has a lot to answer for and I for one am going to wring his neck first and ask questions after!"

Trace yelled out the last word so that it ricocheted like a gunshot. Agnes winced from the sound. The Colonel grunted in agreement. And the disc began to glow. The disk and the dome came alive with a wash of blue, as though the sky had entered the inside of the mountain. Agnes felt movement under her feet.

Agnes cried out. "The disc...it's moving!"

"Get to the center." Trace called to the other two.

Agnes and the Colonel made their way on quavering legs, to the center of the disc where Trace was standing. They stood there as the disc began to ascend at an alarming rate. From what Agnes could see there was no discernible machinery, simply a column of pulsating light interspersing and illuminating their entire inner world inside the mountain. They rose higher and Agnes could feel her ears pop. Then the disc began to slow.

Trace was amazed. "I guess he heard my request for an elevator...good 'ol Noth! Welcome to the upper floor lady and gentleman. Here you'll find men's underwear, cookware, ancient artifacts and weirdness."

The disc stopped as smoothly as it had started. Another thin stone walkway led out from the disc toward a doorway cut into the side of the peak of the mountain. Still tethered to one another, the three made their way toward the small door. In the center of the door was a keyhole. Trace grinned as he pulled out the Guidestone.

"I think you will love this apartment Mr. And Mrs. Colonel, well priced with a good view..."

"Just open the fucking door already!" The Colonel snapped.

Trace stopped suddenly, the grin fading from is face. "Sure...Colonel. Just trying to lighten the mood..."

Trace placed the key in the hole and another door did the vanishing trick. A cold blast of winter air assaulted them from outside. Trace stepped through to investigate and nearly stepped off the side of the mountain.

"Holy Shit!" He fell to his knees, the tethering line pulling the others forward. "I think we have a problem." He called back. Trace crawled his way back to the safe side of the door.

The Colonel grabbed his jacket to help pull him back. "What's the matter?"

"I think we may need your climbing equipment after all."

Agnes carefully took a look through the doorway. Beyond was a sheer drop down through clouds to some unfathomable depth beyond. She looked off to the left of the doorway and saw the problem. A walkway, that was supposed to connect the doorway with steps leading up to a flat peak, had been sheared away, probably from an avalanche or extreme weather, Agnes couldn't tell which.

"I'll go and get the keystone and bring it back." Trace said, reaching into the Colonel's pack for the rest of the climbing equipment.

Agnes, for some reason she couldn't quite figure out right now, didn't like the idea of Trace out there, all alone.

"No way you are going alone."

"Doesn't that seem like the smart thing to do? Why risk all our lives? What do you think Colonel?"

"Never mind what he thinks, with all due respect Colonel, you have no idea what might happen up there. Remember Red Land where everything disintegrated? Or what if the mountain disappears or anything...no way, we all stay together, you hear me?"

The Colonel turned to Trace. "She's right, Anderson, we don't know what will happen up there. We should stay together."

Trace shook his head, sure that the Colonel would agree with him. The girl wins again. He threw up his arms in defeat.

"Fine. We all go. I'll go first, then Agnes then you Colonel."

In twenty minutes they had arranged the equipment and Trace headed out as lead climber leaving Agnes and the Colonel to follow the protection he anchored to the rock face to secure the safety rope. It was slow going. All three of them had various experience, none more so than Trace, which is why he went first.

He had been climbing all his life, his father was an expert and taught Trace everything he knew. The times spent climbing with his father were some of the best memories he had. Way more fun than this. Agnes came second. She was agile, and strong and had done a fair amount of rock climbing, but nothing like this. She found herself humming 'Ba-Ba Blacksheep' over and over again as she climbed. It somehow calmed her nerves.

Below her, the Colonel was moving with efficiency and grace that belied his age. He seemed right at home, making his way up the mountain, his jaw clenched in grim determination. The three weren't climbing up so much as across and up toward a small clearing above where the destroyed path had lead to. Agnes passed by several anchor points along the way that had connected the pathway to the mountain. How Noth got it up here was beyond her.

They neared the top. Trace arrived and stepped onto the clearing. There was little space at the top, and it seemed to be mostly occupied by a carved rock. As Agnes got closer she could see a flat landing about eight feet in diameter. In the center of the circle stood a column of rock above which floated a keystone radiating a brilliant blue light into the sky.

Trace pulled Agnes the rest of the distance and helped her to a standing position, then reached over to help the Colonel as he arrived. Agnes's breath caught in her throat as she took in the view for the first time. The peak of the mountain stabbed out from a bed of cottony clouds that rolled outwards in all directions towards the horizon.

Agnes felt like she was standing on top of the world. The air was cold but was surprisingly still compared to the wind that buffeted them on the climb. Agnes turned to watch the Colonel arrive; the circle of rock was becoming surprisingly crowded with the three of them. Trace undid his tether, leaving the Colonel and Agnes tied together by a length of rope, then the Colonel came to stand by Agnes.

"Okay Trace, get that thing, then let's get out of here." The Colonel shouted across the circle.

He stood about an arms length from Agnes. Agnes looked worn out from the climb, but her eyes were glowing that favorite glow of mine, full of life and determination.

The Colonel looked surprisingly energized even after the taxing climb.

Trace walked over to the column of rock over which floated the keystone, playing out the scenes in the mountain that had led to this moment. Something didn't feel right to him, but he couldn't put his finger on it. Trace hesitated grabbing the keystone for a moment, sifting through the details looking for something that seemed out of place.

"What's wrong?" It was Agnes. Trace looked over to the concern and questions in her eyes. "I just want to take my time, think it through...it might be booby-trapped".

"Do you honestly think Noth would make someone go to all this trouble just kill them now? For the love of Pete Anderson, grab it and let's get out of here."

Trace turned back to the keystone and wrapped my hands around it. As it came free from it's forcefield, thoughts clicked together like puzzle pieces in his head.

Anderson. In all the years he had known the Colonel, he had never called him by his last name. Now twice he had done so in the space of a few hours. Trace couldn't believe he had missed the pieces, he had seen the same thing in a stranger a couple of days ago. The Colonel had been compromised. He whirled around in time to see the Colonel with a gun in his hand pointing at Agnes's head. Her eyes were filled with terror at the strange turn of events.

"Hand that over to me and I will kill her quickly."

The voice that came out of the Colonel had his sound but was not his. Trace thought furiously trying to make a plan to get through this mess. He stalled for time.

"I should have seen it, Colonel, old friend. I guess I am really tired after all...calling me Anderson was a stupid mistake... Colonel. Or should I call you Krynos?"

At that, Trace watched as the Colonel winced with pain. Suddenly there was a struggle of epic proportions going on inside the old man. Trace walked a few steps closer stepping over the loop of their rope tether, then stopping.

"Yeah, and the Colonel would never have barked at me the way you did. No, the man I know as the Colonel is a good man that loves my stupid sense of humour."

The Colonel winced again in pain. This time harder. Trace hated to cause him to be tortured like this, but could see no other choice. He cast a quick glance at Agnes then down at my feet wrapped inside the loop of the tether, hoping like hell she could get a sense of what he was trying to do, and what he needed from her.

Trace continued his taunting, trying to push the creature in the Colonel as hard as he could.

"And that last show of Viagra strength as you climbed up here like a spring chicken, I should have caught that, for sure."

Another wince, this time bigger than before, the gun wavered in the Colonel's hand for a moment. Trace pushed on.

"So...Krynos...you mind if I call you Kry? You got a real Napoleon complex, huh? Noth told me you were some little man who didn't get laid enough and took it out on everyone else. Yeah, you tiny-dicked wonder, need to push around people to get a hard on do ya?"

Trace started laughing,

"Your not even a real man, just a freaky ghost loser that just can't figure out that your grand plans are as useless as your limp ghost dick. No wonder that had to put you away with this."

Trace held up the keystone for him to see then in one swift move pretended to hurl it over the side of the mountain in the best football deek he could muster.

The Colonel cried out in pain and frustration as his eyes looked to where he thought Trace had thrown it. Trace took that moment to reach down and grab the rope at his feet, looping it over an outcrop of rock.

Agnes had figured out his gambit. She threw herself with all her strength into the Colonel who careened sideways then teetered off the edge of the mountain. He was still attached to Agnes, however and as he fell the rope lost slack and pulled her over as well. Trace grabbed on with everything he had. By the time they stopped moving they were both dangling over the side of the mountain by a rope that was looped around an outcrop of rock and wrapped around Trace's waist.

Nice. Just the kind of adventure Trace looked for in a holiday. His feet were anchored as best as they could be on the rock of the disc. Agnes was screaming in terror ten feet below the peak.

"Agnes! Listen to me! You have to climb up. I can't hold you too much longer. Climb up. Come on Agnes you can do it."

Agnes quelled her screaming and there was silence. Trace could feel from the other end of the rope that the Colonel was also struggling to make it back up, but when he fell he fell head first and he spent precious moments trying to upright himself. He snarled ferociously and Trace knew that somehow Krynos was feeding him energy and trying to fight the Colonel's resistance.   He only needed to hold out against Krynos for a few moments more to buy Agnes the time she needed.

"Come on Agnes. You can do it." Trace coaxed.

Agnes screamed back "Just shut up for a moment, I'm trying."

The strain against Trace's body was almost too much to bear, in a moment he was sure he would lose his grip and his footing and lose them both and probably him in the process. Suddenly, to Trace's right, Agnes's hand appeared on the rope at the edge of the peak, then another hand followed the first as she pulled her body over the top, sprawling on the ground breathing heavily.

Now came the hard part for Trace. The Colonel had begun to climb up the rope and Trace could feel him straining. He had no choice but to let go and end it. But this was the Colonel, his second father, a man who had looked out for me all his life. Trace owed him so much, how could he just let him go? From below came more snarling as the Colonel fought for control over Krynos.

Trace called out. "Please Colonel, you can win this. Fight him, dammit!"

There was silence for a moment, then through the mountain air a thin voice called out to Trace. A voice wracked with pain, one that had reached the end.

"Trace? Trace! Please Trace, please...you must let me go...I can't hold him off much longer...so strong...please...Son, let me go."

Hearing his voice, Trace looked over the edge to see the Colonel his hands clenched around the rope in pain, struggling to keep climbing and let go at the same time, creating a strange agonizing stalemate in a battle of wills.

The Colonel's face was ragged from his struggle, a struggle Trace knew he was going to lose. Tears streamed down Trace's face as he watched him, so strong, as he had been his whole life, fighting this last battle. The Colonel looked up at him, his voice a hoarse shout.

"Give my regards to your father."

Then he smiled and nodded. Trace let go of the rope and watched one of his childhood heroes drop into the clouds.

Agnes watched the scene with mute horror. A cry stuck in her throat as Trace let go of the rope. She could only imagine the horrendous cost to him. She watched him sit back and stare into the empty space where the Colonel had been. He was the picture of grief and her heart ached to witness it.

She turned away, distracted by a soft crackling sound from behind her. The column that once held the keystone was now a blinding slash of white light, she shielded her eyes as the light dimmed to a tolerable level. She looked back to see within the light the image of Noth beckoning to her and Trace. The gesture was urgent. Agnes got to her feet.

"Come on. We have to go," She said.

He didn't move. She went over to him and kneeled down beside him and gathered his face in her hands gently moving into his field of vision.

"Come...on! There is no time. Make his death mean something. Let's go finish this. NOW!"

Trace took a deep breath as awareness came back to his pain stricken eyes. He searched her face intently for a moment as though recording it, his hand gently brushing the hair from her eyes. He smiled, his boyish grin lightening his features.

Agnes, felt like her heart was going to break for him. She wanted to hold him and take his pain away, but she resisted, instead letting out a grunt and standing up grabbing his hand in the process and lugging him up to his feet. Trace followed Agnes toward the light, retrieving the last Keystone that had fallen to the ground a short distance away. Agnes let go of his hand as they approached the portal, took a deep breath and stepped through. Trace looked back one last time at the edge of the cliff. Inside he made a promise to the Colonel. One he intended to keep.

Trace turned away and stepped into the light.

FOURTEEN: Long Ride to Oblivion

"So let's go over the plan again Mr. Noth."

Noth sighed a big alien sigh at Trace, but he wanted their plan to go off as well as possible, with as few injuries as possible. Trace never figured himself for a commando by any stretch of the imagination, but having a military dad and the Colonel in his life taught him a few things.

At the thought of the Colonel, Trace's insides began to well up, but he forced his grief into a tiny corner of himself. He would look at that later.

He looked over at Agnes, intently examining a stun grenade, looking both terrified and intrigued. *And beautiful.* But she couldn't help that, *nothing like a gorgeous girl handling ordinance.*

They had had a couple days of rest while they prepared. Agnes and he, had a different energy between them now. Exactly what that meant was somewhat beyond Trace's ability to analyze at this point, there would be time enough for that later...if there was a later. She looked up for a moment and met his eyes and something tangible passed between them that made her flush. She looked away again. *Perhaps I still had a chance after all.*

Noth's voice pulled Trace back from libido land. "All right Mr. Anderson. Once we are through whatever surprises they may have in store for us, we must triangulate the three stones. This will open a portal into Cha-sos or what you call Chaos. Remember what I told you so many days ago, it was Krynos who discovered the energy and used it for his own purposes. Chaos must remain in check, but not destroyed, for it is essential to the workings of your world. When the three re-contained Cha-sos using the

Keystones they imprisoned Krynos with it...hoping it would be forever."

"But that didn't work out according to plan." Agnes said.

"Precisely." Noth replied.

Trace jumped in, wanting more details than they had been given to this point. "So. How do we destroy Krynos once and for all...that is the plan isn't it?"

"Yes Mr. Anderson. I have not wavered in my resolve to see a permanent end to his interference in this world. Krynos, in his present form, cannot exist outside of Chaos's world. That is why he must find hosts as we know all too well. His energy is leaking out through cracks in the prison that he created over the years.   It was his hope to use the Keystones to open the doors wide, so to speak."

"A prisoner with the keys to his own cell. Free to come and go as he pleases." Agnes said.

Noth nodded. "Yes. With control over the Keystones and the doors wide open he would be all-powerful. Unstoppable, with an endless source of dark energy."

"Chaos" Trace said.

"Precisely. The portal that we will need to open using the Keystones is kind of like a back door, a secret entrance if you will. The plan is to enter the world of Chaos, open the main doors, lure him out, shut and lock those main doors behind him, locking him out, then escape through the back door and close the portal. Krynos cannot exist outside of the world of Chaos. Without the connection, his essence will be destroyed, and Chaos will be contained once more, as it was always meant to be."

"What about the crack he made?" Agnes pointed out.

"That can be repaired and once outside, Krynos cannot re-enter through it."

Trace clapped his hands "Okay, well it all sounds pretty clear and simple enough...not! How should we lure Krynos out?"

Noth turned to him. "With the only thing he cares about."

"And what precisely is that?" Trace asked.

"The energy of Chaos."

"And how do we get that?"

"That, Mr. Anderson, is where you come in. You're going to steal it."

The time had come to see how quickly their half-baked idea would get them killed. They stood in Noth's apartment on a flat paper-thin disk, made from some indiscernible material.

Noth looked at Agnes and Trace as he prepared. "My power is limited. I can only open a gateway for a brief time. Therefore, we must move quickly. I should be able to get us in very close to Krynos's statue in the cavern"

Trace's heart skipped a beat. "Should? What happens if you're off."

"Then we will materialize into solid rock."

Agnes exchanged a worried glance with Trace. Then, they both burst out laughing. Noth watched their mirth with a befuddled expression. Trace gasped for air then struggled to regain his composure. After a moment Agnes and he pulled themselves together.

"Okay. Cool. Sounds like a fun ride," Trace said, then clutched two stun grenades in his hands, put on his sunglasses and hearing protection.

Agnes and Noth did the same. Noth had no weapons, but Agnes was nervously clutching a tranquilizer gun. She cocked the gun and looked determined. *Good enough for me,* Trace thought.

"All right! Let's get going shall we? Noth, fire it up."

Noth closed his eyes and the disk started to glow. A shaft of energy formed around them, and, for a moment,

Trace felt like he had been turned to vapor. Then the solidity of the world crashed back into his senses. He had a moment to register that they had arrived in the right place, before he realized they were surrounded by a group of armed men.

Eight men, all looking grim and determined with guns pointing at Agnes, Trace and Noth. Standing beside the men grinning like an asshole, was the asshole, Eddy.

"Everyone drop your weapons." He screeched. "Do it NOW!" Guns were cocked all around them.

"Well, if it isn't Eddy Smiter." Trace couldn't keep the scorn from tinting his voice and he thought some taunting might just give him an edge, like it did with the Colonel. "Why don't you stop being rude, turn around and show us your face...oh, sorry that is your face, thought it was your asshole."

"Shut the fuck up, big man" Eddie screamed back. Then stood there for a moment looking smug. "Such a big man. Well, big man time for you to die. Then, I'm going to take your bitch here and fuck her."

Trace turned to Agnes. "Not to worry Agnes, you won't feel a thing."

"SHUTUP!" Eddy turned to his men. "Take Anderson over there and kill him Watch the other guy, too. The girl stays with me." Two men made their way over to Trace and grabbed his arms.

"Oh, man Eddy. All this power you've gained and you need to order others to take care of what you're too scared of to take care of yourself." Trace started laughing hard. "What a fucking loser, dude."

Eddy's face darkened into an angry snarl. He stormed over to Trace and backhanded his left cheek, hard. The power in the blow was astonishing coming from such a little guy. Trace was knocked back out of the hands of his restrainers a few feet away, the pain ringing in his head.

"Wow, Eddy, Trace said wiping some blood off the corner of his mouth. "Got some serious steroid program going for you, huh?"

Eddy strode over to trace and grabbed him by his jacket, hoisting him up without effort. His face loomed large in Trace's wavering vision.

"I am powerful! I will kill you myself! I will..."

Suddenly Eddy stopped talking for a moment. A wince of pain flew across his face. His eyes seemed to lose their focus for a moment, but his grip on me remained firm. He released Trace, grabbed his head with a gasp and then stepped back to his men. After taking a moment to catch his breath, Eddy got control over himself.

"Change of plans. It seems Anderson is still useful."

Trace looked back at Noth who nodded imperceptibly while keeping his eyes on Eddy.   Agnes looked pleasantly disgusted at the meager existence that Eddy presented to the world. *So much for worrying about competition.*

Eddy was strutting again, grinning from ear to ear, like he was suddenly stoned out of his mind.

"I will kill you myself Anderson, after I fuck the girl in front of you..."

"So many changes to the program Eddy, I just can't keep up. Why don't you just kill everybody and go fuck yourself...because the thought of seeing you naked is more terrifying than death..."

"SHUT THE FUCK UP!"   Eddy screamed so loud, veins popped out on his forehead.

Trace wondered for a moment whether he could provoke him into an aneurism. What Eddy did next wasn't so funny, however. He reached over and grabbed Agnes, spinning her around so that he was behind her. Eddy then pulled out a knife and held it to her face.

"She's not going to be so pretty in a moment if you don't shut the fuck up. I'd hate to maim her because of you, but her ass will still be as nice as it was."

Trace watched in horror as Eddy's tongue snaked out of his ugly mouth and licked the side of Agnes's neck. Agnes's face was awash with terror, as she looked into my eyes pleading for help.

"Okay, okay Eddy... you win, you win buddy. Please, just leave her alone."

Eddy Cackled. "Oh the big bastard man doesn't like the idea of real man play."

Trace wasn't quite sure what the fuck 'man play' meant, but he went along with it.

"You're right Eddy. I don't like it. And you want to know what's funny? Agnes here doesn't even like me. Hates my frigging guts, would never want to do anything with me. Isn't that right Agnes?"

Tears formed in Agnes's eyes. Then her face took on the look of steel.

"That's right Mr. Anderson, you make me sick." She softened for a moment in Eddy's grip rubbing her hand along Eddy's arm. "I'd rather have Eddy here than you any day or night of the week."

Eddy cackled again and ground his crotch into Agnes's backside. "Ooooh, ya. That's going to be good, yeah!"

Another wince of pain went across Eddy's features. He let go of Agnes. "Okay...now enough chat. You three are going to open the portal for the master and in a few minutes I will be rewarded beyond your wildest imagination. Except you won't be alive to see my rise to glory as Krynos's right hand man."

For the first time, Eddy turned his attention to Noth, who had been patiently waiting. "Set up the Keystones. Unlock the door and let the master come forth. Oh, by the way, Noth. Krynos has some interesting plans for you."

Eddy cackled again. "MOVE!"

Noth removed the pack he was wearing and placed it on the floor. We kneeled down by Noth to help. Eddy ushered his men away, giving the three of us a quick moment.

Noth spoke quickly in a hushed whisper. "Krynos needs us to use the Keystones because we are not linked to him."

"Are you just going to open it for him?" Trace whispered.

"Krynos doesn't actually know how the Keystones work, I'm going to open something but it won't be the front door. Be ready to move. You still have that stun grenade in your pants do you not, Mr. Anderson?"

Trace nodded, not quite sure where Noth was going here, but then since this whole thing started, he never did. Flying by the seat of their pants seemed to work in the past, so why change the trend now?

"Good. Be ready for my signal, when it comes set it off to distract the guards, then run to the center. You both must get there before Eddy. He will try to follow. I will take care of him. Once you are inside you will be disoriented but the bracelets I gave you will help keep you safe. Remember the plan once you are inside, the rest is up to you. You have one hour, then I will open the door."

Eddy came back from instructing his men and scowled at us. "Get on with it, losers."

Noth instructed Agnes and Trace where to stand and how to hold the Keystones. They were about fifteen feet apart in an equilateral triangle. During the set up he had secreted the stun grenade up the sleeve of his jacket. They were ready.

The Keystones rested in the crook of Trace's left arm. He had the red one, Agnes the blue, and Noth the yellow. They hadn't stopped glowing since they had retrieved them, and now in close proximity to one another, they seemed more incandescent than ever. As they finished the triangle,

Noth closed his eyes and the Keystones began to pulsate in a rhythm sympathetically to each other. A static charge seemed to fill the cavern, making the hairs on Trace's arms stand up.

A rainbow of colours began playing off the surface of the rock and on the faces of Eddy's men. He looked over at Eddy, who seemed mesmerized by the dazzling light show. He was grinning furiously, saliva running down his face, such a grotesque little man. Suddenly a slash of black ripped open in the air in the middle of the triangle.

Everything then seemed to happen in slow motion.

Trace saw the look change on Eddy's face, from glee to one of dismay. He started to yell something. Trace let the stun grenade drop into his right hand and with his thumb he pulled the pin. Trace quickly kneeled down and placed the keystone on the floor of the cavern, then took off at a sprint toward the black portal Noth had opened.

Across the triangle, Agnes did the same thing. Trace heard Eddy roar STOP! As he took off toward them, the stun grenade went off as both Agnes and Trace dove into the center of the portal. Trace dove in feet first. Eddy was right behind them, but just as Agnes and Trace were through, Noth closed the portal.

Eddy had been only halfway through when the portal closed, he tried to grab for Trace's hand to pull him in, but he grabbed the bracelet on his wrist, instead, pulling it off, letting it tumble away into the portal. Trace watched his face as the blackness closed around his torso, his legs still in the other world. In that moment, Trace believed, Krynos left Eddy. He fell away from him, watching him die in horror and confusion. He had awakened, just as his life was ending. Then his scream of terror and pain cut off abruptly somewhere behind me as they all tumbled through the black abyss.

Trace arrived into an anarchic world of half-formed ideas like fragments of dreams long forgotten. There was no up or down, everything was utter bedlam. Topsy-turvy. Trace felt like a random article thrown into a hoarder's warehouse. Beneath his feet, he trod upon what seemed to be a fiery orange sky cluttered with broken dreams and incomplete thoughts while above his head floated cluttered images and objects from the world in which he lived. He had been set free into an ever-changing kaleidoscope of reality.

At a thought, the entire world would shift and disorganized itself. A million smells assaulted him, permeated him, bringing with them more discordant thoughts and feelings. The sound of pandemonium snarled at his ears. Trace couldn't hear above the din of voices, half sentences, words, cries, screams, laughter and agony.

The turmoil of all this unruliness permeated him. Separated him. He could feel himself being pulled into an infinite number of unidentifiable pieces, like a billion-piece puzzle thrown into the wind. He had to fight with every fiber of his being to remain whole, to simply retain the concept of the one of himself. His heart was pounding in his disassociated chest a million miles away from where it should be. He wanted to give over and allow himself to simply dissipate into this rat's nest world, where rules had no place, where everything and nothing was possible. He wanted to let go.

A stilling hand clutching a distant shoulder brought him back to himself. Agnes's hand, then the sound of her voice calling his name. "Trace?!" "Trace! Stay with me!" Something slid over his wrist. *Noth's bracelet.* Abruptly the pieces of him congealed back into himself, reforming him; making him whole once again.

The feeling of dissociation seemed to slow as Trace came back from the fragmenting power of chaos. The world was still disorienting, but manageable. Noth's bracelet filtered out the direct exposure of this world.

Agnes was kneeling by his side, looking intently into his eyes. "You all right? She asked, her eyes full of concern.

Trace nodded and breathed deep, trying to purge himself of the unsettling feeling of being pulled apart.

"Yeah, I'm fine. That...that was way worse than magic mushrooms. I felt like I was being ripped to pieces" Trace smiled at her to ease her concern and put on his best surfer dude voice. "Wow, that was trippy dude."

Agnes looked relieved. She glanced around clearly bothered by what she saw, despite the bracelet's nulling effects. Trace got up and helped her to her feet. Movement in this world was like a bad skype call, jerky and disconnected.

"I don't know how long we can take of this place, let's go find the source stone and get out of here."

Agnes was looking behind Trace. "I have a feeling I know where it is."

"Where?"

"There."

Her arm pointed in several directions at once. Trace waited until the arm finally focused on one area in the distance. A spiraling vortex of randomness appeared in the distance, how he missed it at first he wasn't sure. But there it was: the center of all the madness swirling around them. It was a terrifying looking place. Objects, images, and thoughts seemed to spew out at an alarming pace from the center. Near the vortex there was a thin slash in the fabric of the world, the crack created by Krynos. It was pulsating an angry red as though it was fighting for existence.

Trace knew in that moment that from the outside Noth was busy repairing the prison. They stopped and watched the battle unfold in the distance. The tear seemed to quiver in pain as it changed from angry red to deep purple. Like a wound being healed on a monumental scale. In a short while the wound suddenly disappeared. A popping sound reverberated all around them. Then an angry scream rang out filling the air with a shockwave of anger and remorse. A rolling thunder-ball of hate shook the world of Chaos, nearly bringing us to our knees.

"Noth must have sealed the crack from the outside. Krynos is imprisoned once again, it seems." He said.

Agnes looked at him, her eyes full of realized terror. "And so are we. Let's get going."

As they approached the vortex the world became more intense. They waded through the river of humanity. The castoffs of thoughts the possibilities of time bombarded the pair. Scenes would play out all around them, hoards of people would appear screaming and fighting and killing one another, then vanish in a moment. A man sat on a giant rolling pin holding his head in dismay, and then laughing hysterically.

Landscapes would form; mountains grow, then crumble and erode in a breath. Trace found himself thinking of his own life, how all the different parts of it seemed to make up a linear progression, but he knew somehow, that was an illusion. The randomness of life, the chaos, had an important part to play. *If we embraced too much chaos, our lives would be volatile messes, too little and we would stagnate.* Trace was sure that was how this

'rogue energy' as Noth called it, fit in with humans. Chaos had to exist because of who humans were and what they were like. Trace was sure that somewhere there was a world of order to balance this one, full of perfectly made beds and neat rows and columns of things.

Somehow the thought of such a place calmed him, but he couldn't possibly know how to get there. Perhaps he had lived with too much chaos for so long he was beginning to get used to it. Chaos was normal for him. Perhaps that was the problem, why his life always felt so unbalanced. Agnes seemed to be slowing beside him.

"Are you all right?" He asked.

She turned to him, there were cubed tears tumbling down her face.

"I can't go on, Trace. This place is not for me."

She was shivering, her face screwed up in a ball of anxiety. Agnes was a scientist, after all, an archeologist, one who was used to detail and order and putting the pieces together in a logical pattern. Agnes thrived on order and it was no wonder to Trace that this place would be terrifying to a person like her.

He took her hand. "It will be all right Agnes, stick with me. We'll see it through."

It was in this way, two humans walking through the land of chaos, that they met Krynos.

It was a surprising sight, because Trace didn't know what to expect. There, near the vortex, a middle aged man with curly jet black hair that fell in messy heaps around a fine gentle featured face sat quietly on a fragment of a burned out car, his face leaning on his chin, brooding, lost in thought. He was a big man, lean and broad shouldered. At their approach, his head rose and he met Trace's eyes; again, not what Trace had expected. There was a strange gentleness in Krynos's eyes nestled in deep crystal blue, along with a fierce intelligence. He gave both Agnes and Trace a long searching stare as though he was memorizing every detail of their existence.

"Hello Mr. Anderson, Ms. Argwhistle. Kind of you to join me." His voice was gentle, soothing and inviting.

Okay, this was NOT what I had been expecting, Trace thought. Trace was sure that he would be like some gargoyle thing with glowing eyes and a gravelly devil voice, not some put together, handsome slightly older model from an expensive watch ad. Trace looked over at Agnes. She was definitely surprised also. Surprised and he could see by the twinkle in her eyes, intrigued. She took a step toward him. *Great, so I came all this way to have Mr. Beautiful steal my girl.*

This was not the plan at all. Trace figured they could steal the source stone and lure Krynos out the front door with it. Well that had been Noth's plan, but he left out a couple of details, namely how charming and good looking the bastard was. From here on it was winging it time.

Agnes took another step towards him, then spoke, her voice uncertain. "Hello Mr...uhh, Krynos."

A gentle laughter shook Krynos's big frame. The air was filled with vibrations of his mirth, pissing Trace off royally.

"It has been a long time since I have been in the company of a woman. You are delightful."

He glanced over at Trace as he seethed. He smiled again reassuringly.

"Fear not Mr. Anderson, I do not wish to be your rival. In fact, I would be most interested in a partnership."

He stood up then and Trace's body tensed, but Krynos only walked in a wide circle, his hands extending out all around him.

"Welcome to my world: one that I have inhabited for so long, one that I have come to know and understand, one that can provide endless possibilities. You came here expecting a monster, but as you see, I am no monster. My sole purpose has been to bring goodness and peace to your world. With me controlling the forces of Chaos, there need be no more suffering, no more pain. All dreams can come to fruition for your kind."

He stopped then and looked back at his two visitors. His voice filled the air and Trace could feel his resolve crumbling and he wondered if he had been wrong about all of this. If they had all been wrong. Krynos's magnetic voice seemed so calm and rational. Trace watched myself from a distance being sucked into his words, but offered no resistance. *What was the point of that?* Krynos swept his hand above his head looking right at him, seemingly inside of him and closed his eyes.

"Allow me to show you the possible, Mr. Anderson."

In an eye-blink, the world around Trace changed and his reality shifted. He stood in an impossible apartment made from glass on a disc hovering above an idyllic island, green and lush, with pristine beaches surrounding a deep azure ocean. Trace surveyed the view from my balcony and drank in the fresh breeze. How long had he lived here? He couldn't remember, didn't care. He was thirsty. A tall glass appeared in his hand and in a gulp, he emptied it of its cool, sweet liquid, a bracelet on his wrist clinking against the side of the glass as he tipped the glass up. Still thirsty, Trace wanted more, but a call from below distracted him. On the beach, a woman waved her hand up to him. Agnes.

With a thought he joined her on the sand. She wore a deep red short dress, her legs tanned and luxurious, sand squishing through bare feet. She turned her sun kissed face toward him, her hair gently tussled around her beautiful face by the playful wind. Her lips beckoned him and he ached to touch her, to feel her willing body against his own. His need for her grew and he reached out to draw her in, his hand almost touching her face and suddenly Trace's reality shifted again...

...and he was standing in his condominium overlooking a vast city at night, his reaching hand grasping the edge of the balcony, he noticed a bracelet dangling on his wrist. Fireworks danced in the distant sky. Trace called over his shoulder.

"Agnes! Come here and look at this."

He waited patiently while the sky lit up in a dazzling display of colours. He was thirsty. A wine glass appeared in his hand filled with a sparkling gold liquid. Trace emptied the contents feeling the coolness slide down his throat, but somehow not quenching his thirst. The fireworks drew his attention back to the sky.

"Agnes! You're going to miss this."

Trace wondered where she was and in a thought he was in the bathroom. The air was filled with steam and he immediately began to sweat. Water was running in a large glass shower. Trace walked over and pulled open the door. Agnes was standing there, water running over her nakedness. She was not startled by his sudden appearance; only stood there smiling at him as water streamed down her firm, perfect body. Her eyes held a mischievous playfulness.

"Why don't you join me?" She said.

She turned away from me, revealing a heart shaped buttocks that he longed to touch. She looked over her shoulder.

"Care to wash my hair?"

Trace stripped off his clothes and entered the steamy depths of the shower. He could feel her close, yearned for her. He reached out to caress the smooth length of her back...

...and he was suddenly on the terrace of his chalet, high up in the mountains. The air was chilled but the sun was hot. He wore a thick cable knit sweater, jeans and mountain boots. All around the terrace was a blanket of white capped mountains, stretching as far as the eye could see. Trace was reaching toward a camera and as he grasped it and brought it up to his eyes, a bracelet tapped against the case. He hesitated for a moment as he looked at the bracelet. *When did I get that? Who gave it to me?* He wondered. Something teased at his memory, tickling me with unfamiliar familiarity.

"Don't you want a picture of me?"

At the sound of Agnes's voice, Trace turned. She was wearing a skin tight, black ski outfit, the material hugging her sleek curves. Trace was thirsty. A steaming cup of blue liquid appeared in his hand. He took a sip careful not to burn his lips, but ending up gulping the contents down.

"I'm not going to stand here forever, you know, I'd like to go back in and...get warm." Agnes arched her eyebrow with challenging suggestiveness. Trace clicked off a couple of pictures, her body slinking in mock model poses as she giggled. He laughed also, but was thirsty. Another cup of the steaming blue liquid appeared and he drank it back. He hesitated again, seeing the bracelet on his wrist.

"Are you coming or what?" Agnes reached up and pulled the zipper on her top down. Firm breasts spilled out, nipples astonished by the cool air enticed his vision. Trace put the camera down, the bracelet dropping over the top of his hand. He stared at it and for a moment felt a dizzying rush of vertigo wash over him.

"Come on, Trace...I'm getting...cold." Trace looked back at Agnes and hesitated. The gritty feel of wrongness entered his guts. He wanted Agnes. Ached to touch her, yet somehow he felt that if he took a step toward her, he would get no closer to her. He felt like a fish on a hook, teased and played, but never brought out of the water. He was a plaything, a toy, but not to Agnes.

"Come on Trace."

He looked over at Agnes and he was inside suddenly. She was laying on a sheepskin rug on the floor, naked, firelight dancing over her pristine skin. Her mouth was full and she was breathing heavily, wanting me with her eyes. Trace's body jerked toward her without his volition. He forced myself to stop moving though and fought his bodies desire to go to Agnes and plunge himself deep inside of her.

He was so thirsty, and the bracelet at his wrist was growing tighter, pinching his wrist, digging into his flesh. He screamed in agony and clawed at his wrist, pulling at it until it finally released and flung across the room toward Agnes falling beside her where she lay on the floor.

Agnes looked down at the bracelet for a moment, then reached over and picked it up, curiosity the desire for recognition wrinkling her brow. She held up her own wrist. On it was the identical bracelet. Her eyes went wide with terror as understanding seemed to come to her and she screamed out to him as though from a million miles away.

"No, Trace, No!!!"

The vision of the Chalet wavered. To Trace's left, a swirling vortex appeared, within it's depths he could sense a dark presence. His memory abruptly returned, and with it a seething anger filled him. He had been violated, his feelings for Agnes exploited. Both of them, used, manipulated. Darkness filled him, a black anger he had never quite felt before rocked his whole being. With a roar he dove toward the vortex, he could hear Agnes's voice coming from what seemed a vast distance yelling for him to stop. Trace jumped into the maelstrom and entered Chaos.

Trace arrived in a vast landscape of white. A blank canvas. No up or down, simply white, everywhere.

Krynos was there, Trace could sense his presence all around him. This had been his place for thousands of years. His knowledge of it was intimate. But now Trace was spoiling for a fight and he had gone to the enemies turf to get it. Never the wisest choice, but he was committed. He could feel Krynos's essence circling him like a predator waiting for the kill.

The attack came suddenly, from a hundred different places at once. Trace's entire being was bombarded with images, sensations and emotions. Debris, bits of broken things crashed into me, while at the same time horrifying disfigurements of past life assaulted him. The Colonel, his body broken, his face bloody, accusing of killing him.

Then, his father, an ancient old man melting in a wheelchair in his home, his arms reaching out to Trace for help he could not give.

Agnes appeared, a multitude of men raping her as she screamed out for help and was then swept away from his reach.

Countless faces and moments from his past, twisted truths, ripping at his conscious. He was bleeding from the inside and out.

He tried to lash out, to fight back but Krynos was elusive. He toyed with Trace both physically and mentally. Somehow he knew that he had to find a way to fight him on his own terms, or die here. He started to run, the world of chaos trying to pull him in a million different directions. He struggled to remain whole, to stay together rather than be pulled apart.

A chunk of stone flew out of the white void and crashed into his shoulder, while inside his mind his mother shot herself with a gun she found in his trailer. Absurd things, that couldn't possibly be, but Trace felt them as though they were real. He wrapped his arms around himself and kept running, desperately trying to keep himself from flying apart into a million pieces. It occurred to him as his damage increased that he didn't know where he could possibly be running. He knew in an instant that this was exactly what Krynos was driving him to do. The alternative terrified him, but he knew that if he didn't act quickly, he would be dead. He gathered his courage, and forced himself to stop. His heart was pounding through his chest. Trace looked up and saw a rusted marine barge barreling down on his position. In a moment he would be crushed. Trace ignored the threat. Instead, he took a deep breath, then let himself go.

Instantly, Trace flew into a million pieces, his awareness and presence was suddenly everywhere at once, his physical body...disappeared. He couldn't explain it, nor did he try to. Trace allowed himself to act on instinct alone.

Around him and through him Krynos swirled and he could sense his frustration at losing his quarry.

Game on old man.

Both men searched for pieces of each other and when they encountered them they lashed out. Trace found fragments of Krynos's memory, glimpses of his frustrations and failures of loves long since dead. Trace hurled himself at them, twisting them and torturing them as he had done to him. Trace wasn't proud of his accomplishments, he was simply fighting, clawing his in any way possible for survival.

After a time, Trace began to notice that there was an energy source outside of them that was fueling their frantic battle. He realized that unconsciously, he had been drawing from it, shoring up his defenses, charging his offensive moves against his enemy. A small part of him started to seek out the source of that power, the center of the vortex of chaos.

Suddenly, he had it. An intense pinpoint of power. The Sourcestone. Gathering some more parts of himself, Trace raced toward it. At the same time, Krynos felt his direction and followed after him.

They both arrived at the center at the same time, the many parts of themselves catching up to them to complete the whole. A glowing ember radiating power filled Trace's vision. He reached out for it at the exact same time as Krynos.

The two locked wills as their hands connected with the stone. Both of them, pulled in a tempestuous struggle for dominance. Locked in a Tug of war of wills, Trace fought against Krynos with everything he was made of. Krynos seemed to match him power for power. They stood there, deadlocked for what seemed an eternity, trapped in the prison of Chaos.

Then the door to Chaos opened.

A silver slash appeared in the air above them. Trace knew in that instant that Noth had opened the prison from outside. Krynos hesitated for a moment, a brief moment where he smelled the promise of his freedom.

In that moment Trace attacked him with everything he had. Krynos was caught off guard and not able to recover. His hand flew off the Sourcestone for a moment and the total power of chaos filled Trace. He hurled himself at Krynos and his essence rebounded toward the exit.

Kryno's face was a mask of terror and hatred as he realized, too late, Noth's plan. With one last push Krynos fell through the opening. His scream of anguish was ended as the entrance shut, and he disappeared forever.

The power of Chaos still coursed through Trace. It lured him with its seductive promise. He realized with this power what he could accomplish, what good he could bring to the world. With this power, he could remake the world in a better image. he could become unstoppable. *Like Krynos.*

That thought, a cold splash of realization, stopped Trace's racing mind. What he held in his hand was not for any human. It belonged to all and would be held by no one. It would destroy anyone who thought to play with its reckless, destructive power. Trace thought of Agnes and allowed his love *yes love* for her to give him the extra strength he needed.

Trace walked back to the center of the vortex and placed the stone back in its resting place. In that moment, somewhere, Agnes replaced the bracelet over his physical body and Trace felt himself slipping back into his reality. The world went black. And then for a long while, there was nothing.

<\>

Trace awoke in his trailer. Something was tickling his face. He opened his eyes slowly to see Agnes looking down at him, her hair teasing his cheek. Thoughts and words came to him, but for a long while he did not speak, simply drank her in, hoping that she was real. After a while, he dared to speak.

"Hello." Trace's voice was a croaking mess.

Agnes smiled then. "Thought I lost you." She ran her hand across his cheek. "You okay?"

Trace nodded. Then looked around at the familiar comfort of his home. "How..?"

"When you came back to me, Noth had opened the back door and I pulled you back out of Chaos. He sealed it back up permanently."

"What did you see in there, Agnes?"

"Everything. The beach, the apartment..."

"The shower?"

Agnes blushed and turned her head away. "Yes."

"I'm sorry." Trace said. Somehow, he felt like he had taken advantage of her, though the idea was absurd. It was Krynos who drew them into the fantasy...but the fantasy was based on his feelings, his desires. "It was like being in a dream...and the things I felt for you...I'm sorry."

Agnes kept her face turned away.

"I'm not sorry." She said quietly. "It was a beautiful dream, you dreamed. I felt those things too."

Agnes got up abruptly and busied herself pretending to clean.

"Where is Noth?" Trace asked.

"Gone. Along with the statue and any evidence that it was ever there. There were men, Eddy's men, wandering around the cavern looking lost and bewildered, not sure how they got there. When they saw us they came over to help. We got everyone out and just in time it seems. The entire cavern collapsed. There's nothing left but a pile of dirt where the hole had been.

She smiled then, giving up the pretend cleaning, and came back to sit next to Trace on the bed. She turned and looked at him, her big blue eyes drawing him in. "Sorry we ruined your sandbox, Trace."

He looked at her and smiled, his fingers rising up to gently trace her jaw. "Hey. You called me Trace. You got a thing for me or something?"

She laughed softly as he pulled her in close, their mouths meeting, hungry for more...

Thank You For Reading!

I wrote this a couple of summers ago, with the goal of creating a fun adventure, something to kill an afternoon at the beach with, and hopefully, a series with Trace Anderson, our hero, as he adventures and explores. If you would be so kind as to send along a review, I would be eternally grateful.

All the best
Andrew Dolha

www.ingramcontent.com/pod-product-compliance
Lightning Source LLC
Chambersburg PA
CBHW050944120626
46552CB00001B/380